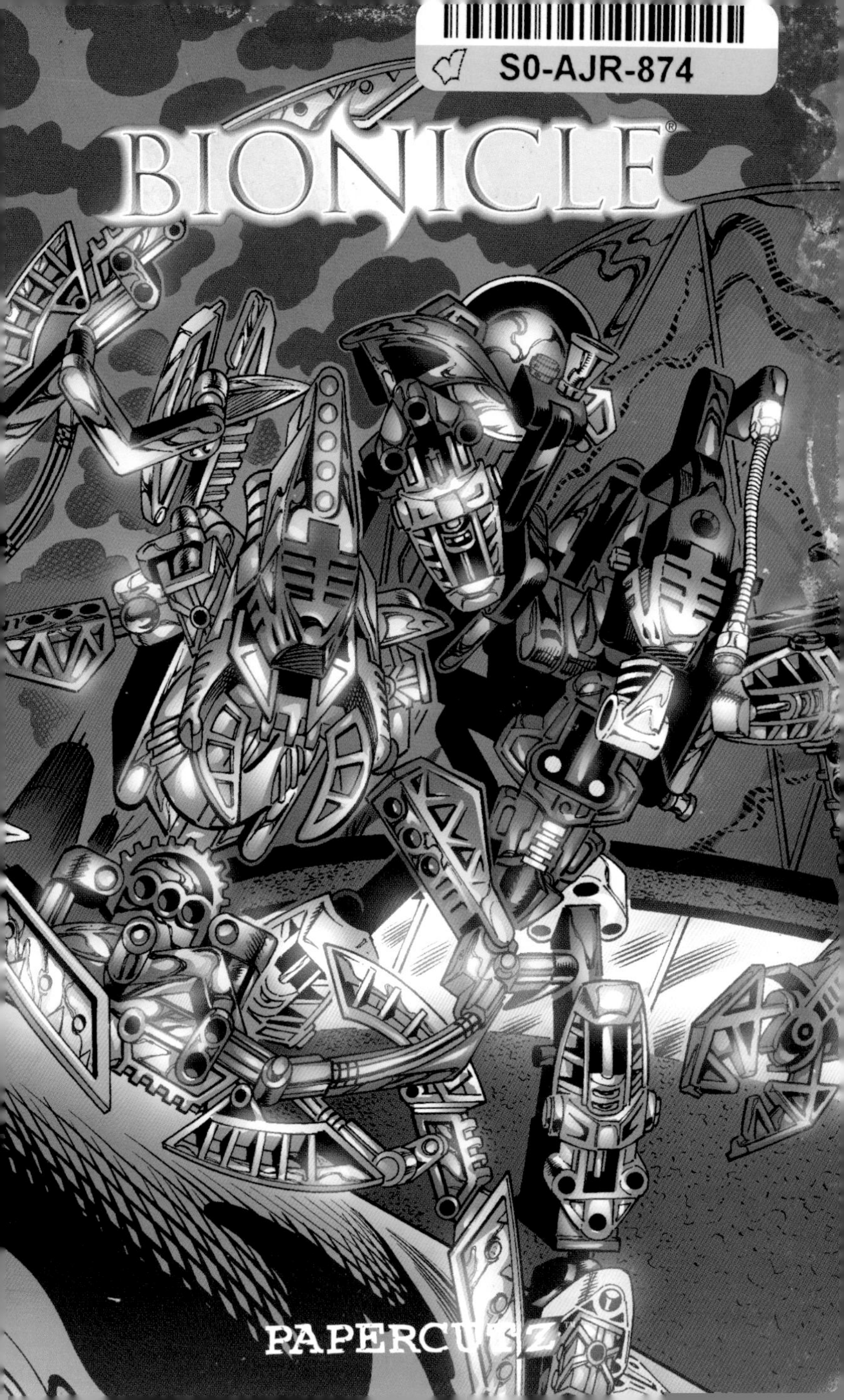

BIONICLE®
PAPERCUTZ

City of Legends

GREG FARSHTEY – Writer
RANDY ELLIOTT, RAY KRYSSING — Artists
TOBY DUTKIEWICZ – Comics Layout and Design
JUSTIN LAMB – Tahtorak Design
PETER PANTAZIS — Colorist
KEN LOPEZ – Letterer
JAYE GARDNER – Original Editor
JOHN McCARTHY – Production
MICHAEL PETRANEK – Editorial Assistant
JIM SALICRUP
Editor-in-Chief

ISBN 10: 1-59707-121-8 paperback edition
ISBN 13: 978-1-59707-121-5 paperback edition
ISBN 10: 1-59707-122-6 hardcover edition
ISBN 13: 978-1-59707-122-2 hardcover edition
LEGO, the LEGO logo and BIONICLE are trademarks of the LEGO Group. Manufactured
and distributed by Papercutz under license from the LEGO Group.
© 2000, 2001, 2008 The LEGO Group. All rights reserved.
Originally published as comicbooks by DC Comics as BIONICLE #16-21.
Editorial matter © 2008 Papercutz.
Printed in China.
Distributed by Macmillan.
10 9 8 7 6 5 4 3 2 1

CITY OF LEGENDS
CHAPTER ONE

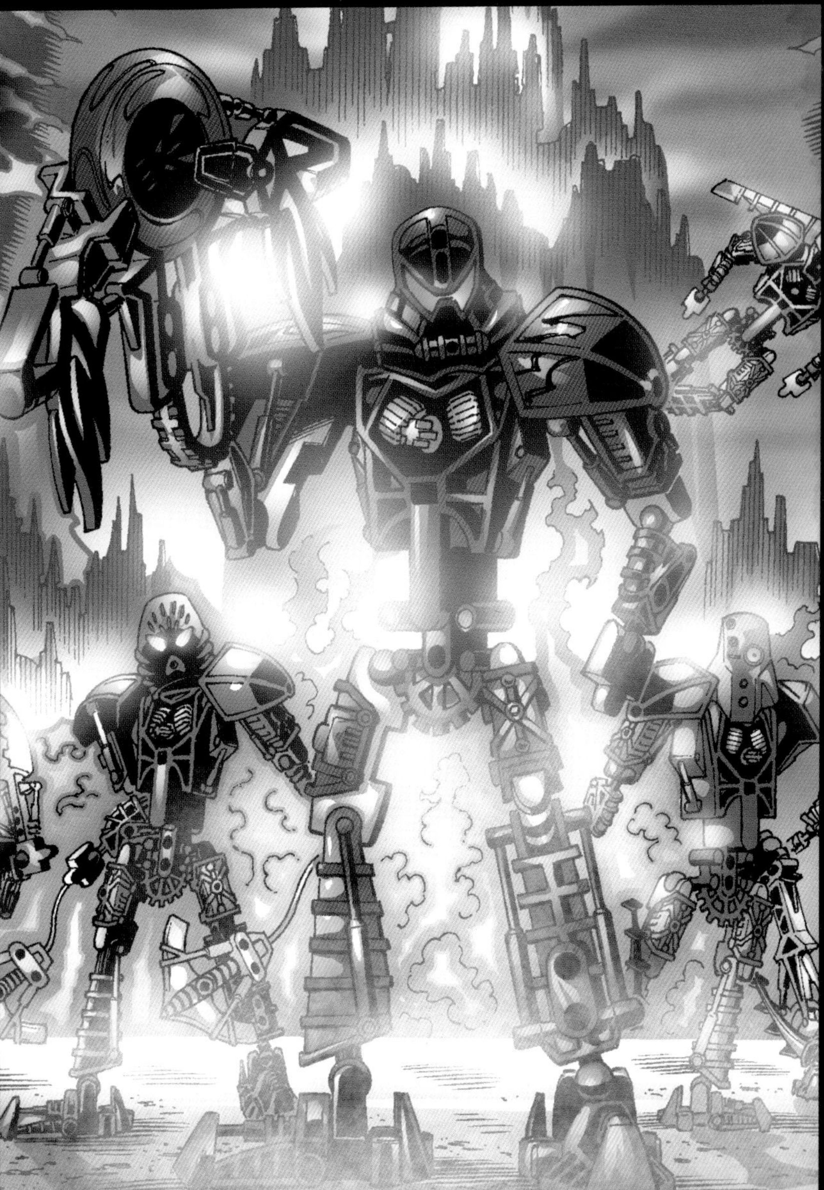

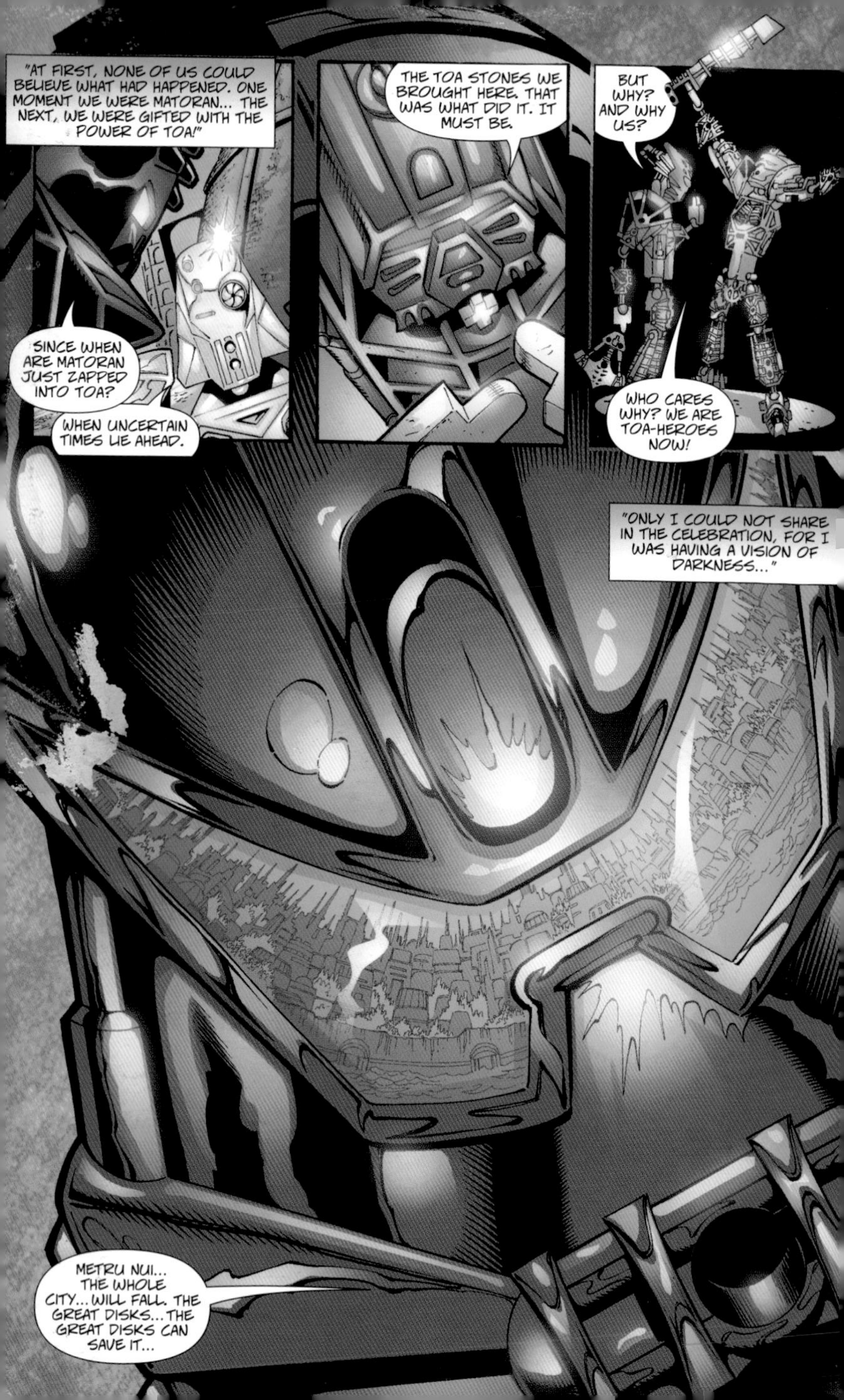
"AT FIRST, NONE OF US COULD BELIEVE WHAT HAD HAPPENED. ONE MOMENT WE WERE MATORAN... THE NEXT, WE WERE GIFTED WITH THE POWER OF TOA!"
SINCE WHEN ARE MATORAN JUST ZAPPED INTO TOA?
WHEN UNCERTAIN TIMES LIE AHEAD.
THE TOA STONES WE BROUGHT HERE. THAT WAS WHAT DID IT. IT MUST BE.
BUT WHY? AND WHY US?
WHO CARES WHY? WE ARE TOA-HEROES NOW!
"ONLY I COULD NOT SHARE IN THE CELEBRATION, FOR I WAS HAVING A VISION OF DARKNESS..."
METRU NUI... THE WHOLE CITY... WILL FALL. THE GREAT DISKS... THE GREAT DISKS CAN SAVE IT...

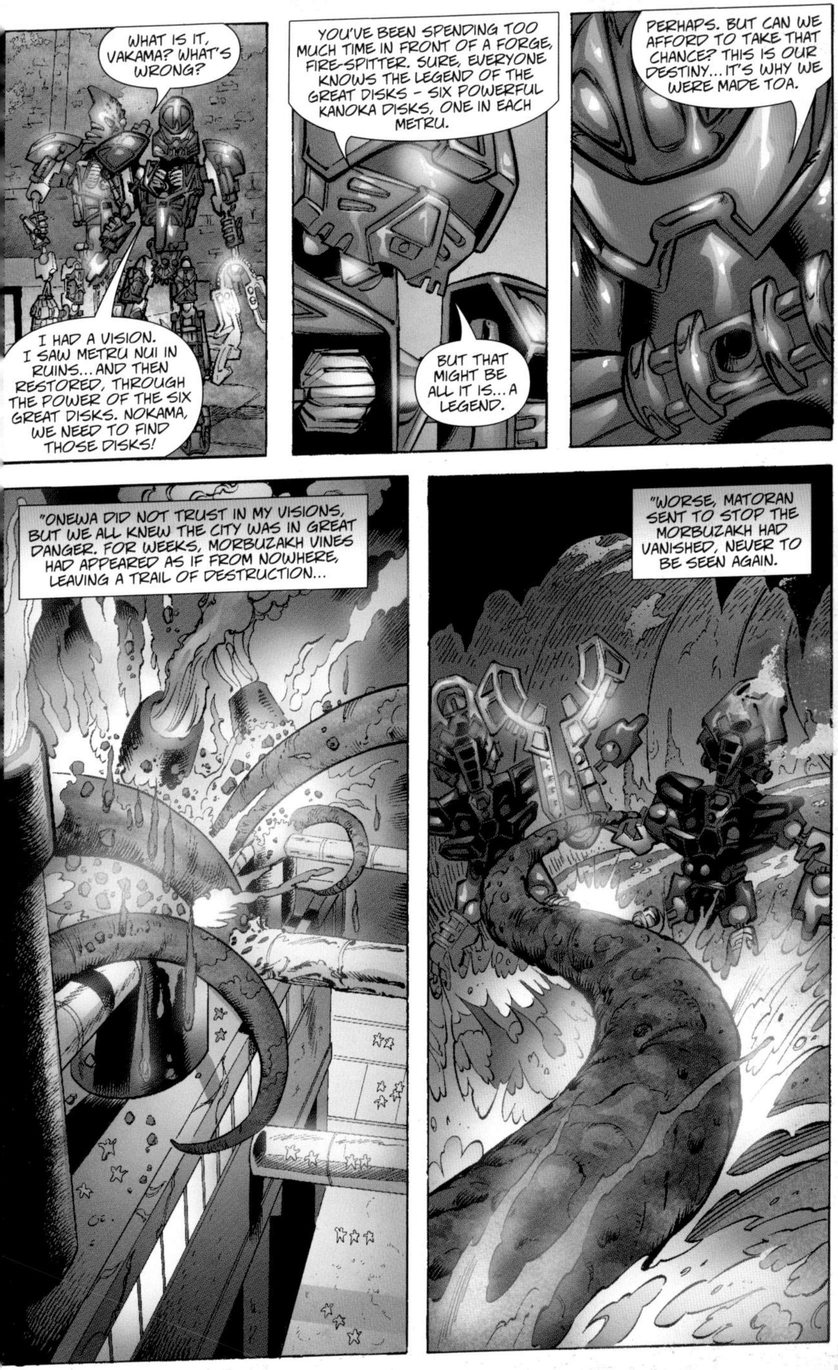
WHAT IS IT, VAKAMA? WHAT'S WRONG?
I HAD A VISION. I SAW METRU NUI IN RUINS... AND THEN RESTORED, THROUGH THE POWER OF THE SIX GREAT DISKS. NOKAMA, WE NEED TO FIND THOSE DISKS!
YOU'VE BEEN SPENDING TOO MUCH TIME IN FRONT OF A FORGE, FIRE-SPITTER. SURE, EVERYONE KNOWS THE LEGEND OF THE GREAT DISKS - SIX POWERFUL KANOKA DISKS, ONE IN EACH METRU.
BUT THAT MIGHT BE ALL IT IS... A LEGEND.
PERHAPS. BUT CAN WE AFFORD TO TAKE THAT CHANCE? THIS IS OUR DESTINY... IT'S WHY WE WERE MADE TOA.
"ONEWA DID NOT TRUST IN MY VISIONS, BUT WE ALL KNEW THE CITY WAS IN GREAT DANGER. FOR WEEKS, MORBUZAKH VINES HAD APPEARED AS IF FROM NOWHERE, LEAVING A TRAIL OF DESTRUCTION...
"WORSE, MATORAN SENT TO STOP THE MORBUZAKH HAD VANISHED, NEVER TO BE SEEN AGAIN.

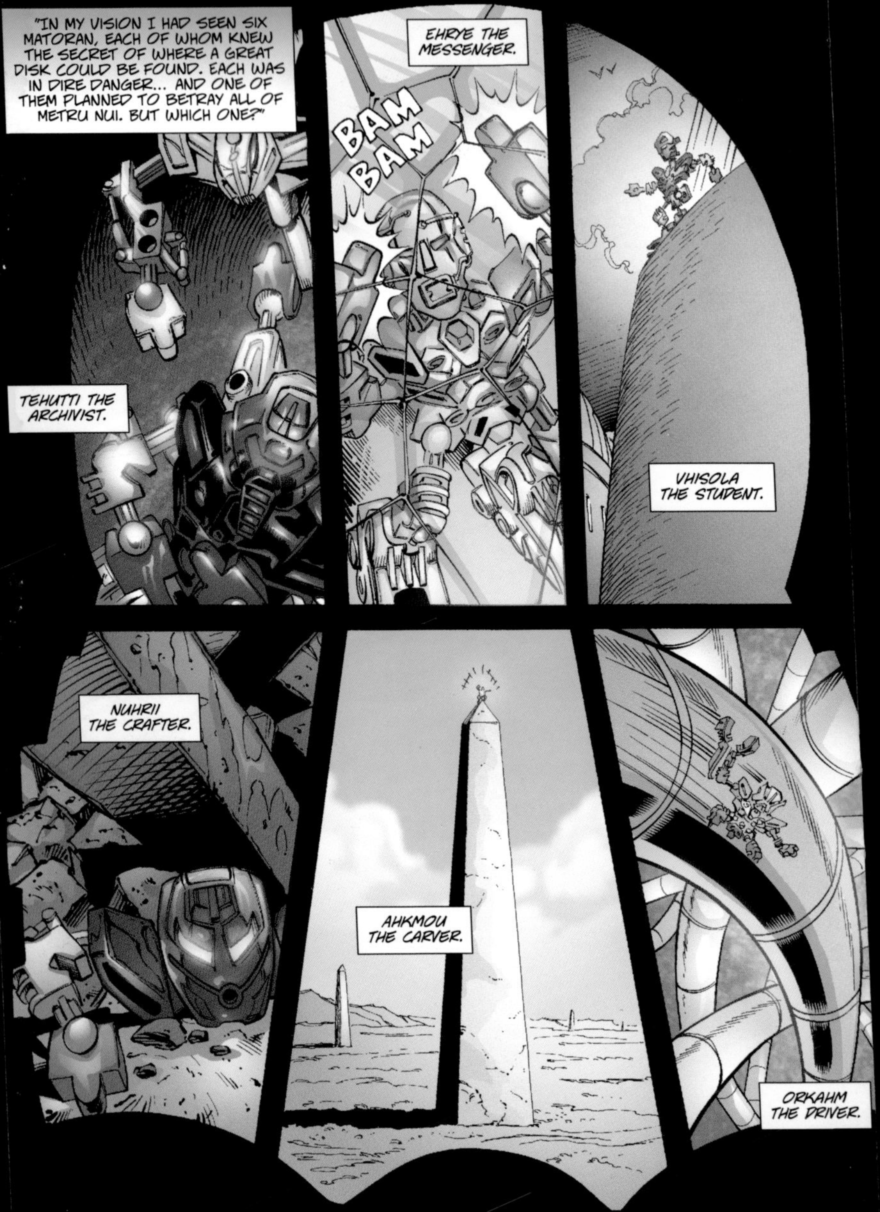
"IN MY VISION I HAD SEEN SIX MATORAN, EACH OF WHOM KNEW THE SECRET OF WHERE A GREAT DISK COULD BE FOUND. EACH WAS IN DIRE DANGER... AND ONE OF THEM PLANNED TO BETRAY ALL OF METRU NUI. BUT WHICH ONE?"
TEHUTTI THE ARCHIVIST.
EHRYE THE MESSENGER.
BAM BAM
VHISOLA THE STUDENT.
NUHRII THE CRAFTER.
AHKMOU THE CARVER.
ORKAHM THE DRIVER.

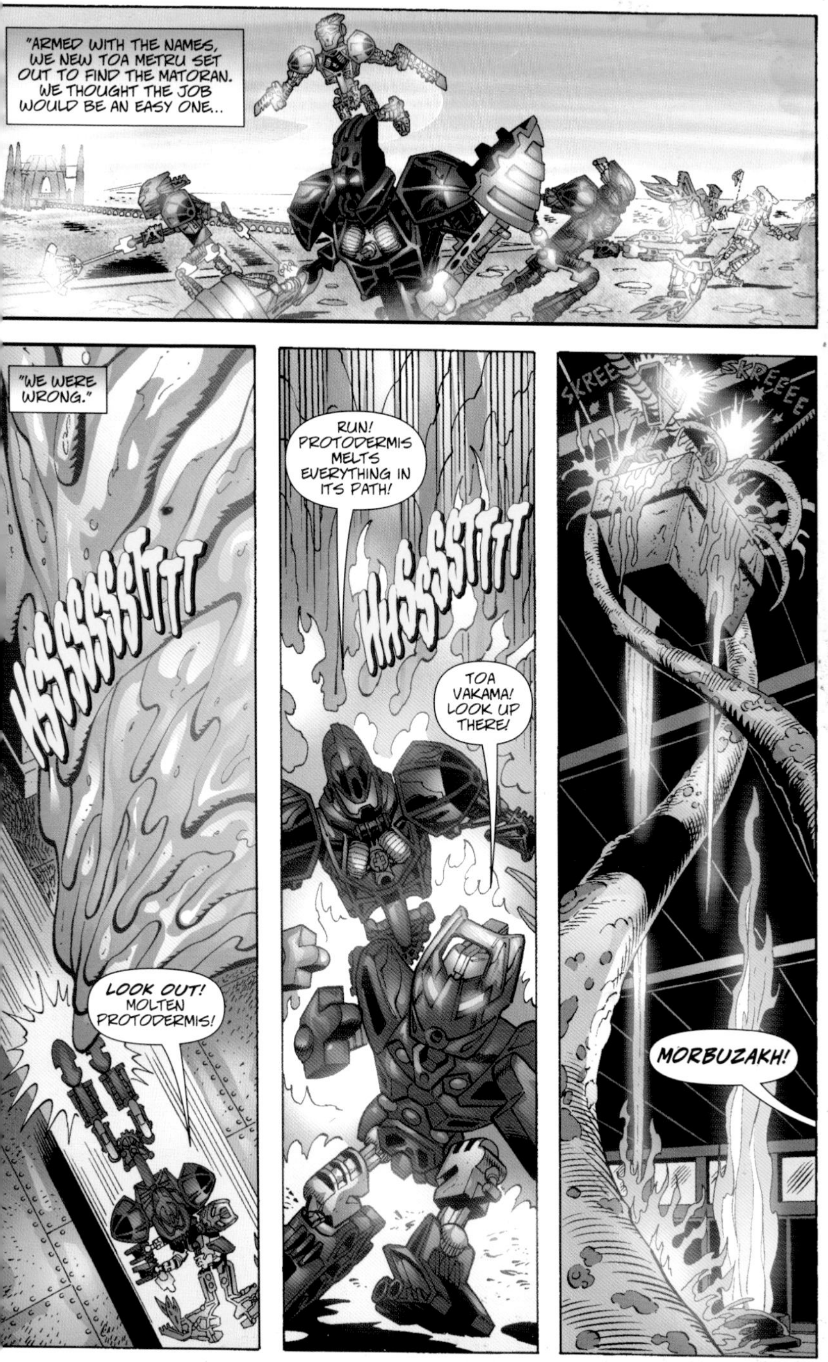
"ARMED WITH THE NAMES, WE NEW TOA METRU SET OUT TO FIND THE MATORAN. WE THOUGHT THE JOB WOULD BE AN EASY ONE...
"WE WERE WRONG."
HSSSSSSTTTT
LOOK OUT! MOLTEN PROTODERMIS!
RUN! PROTODERMIS MELTS EVERYTHING IN ITS PATH!
HHSSSSTTTTT
TOA VAKAMA! LOOK UP THERE!
SKREEE
SKREEEEE
MORBUZAKH!

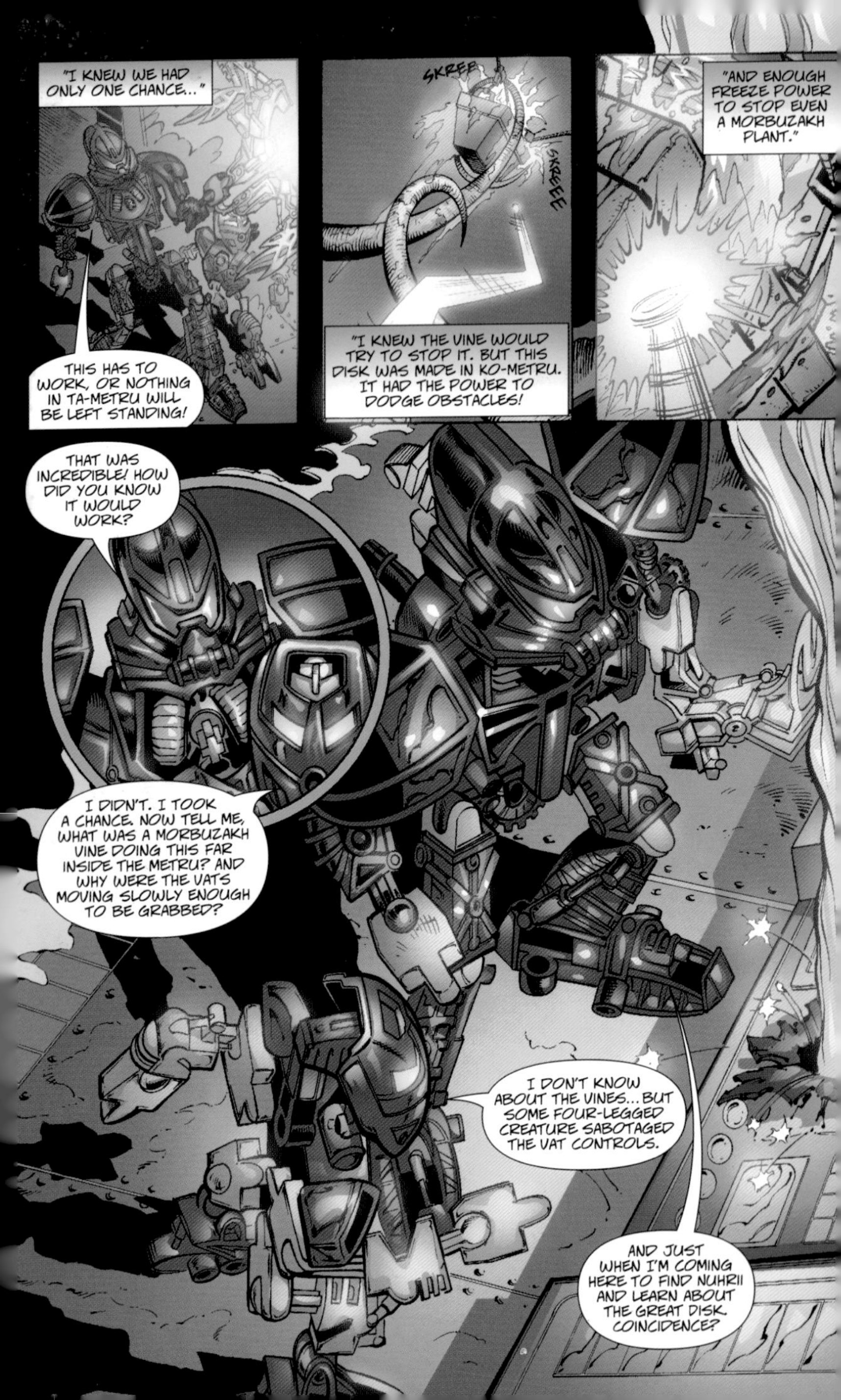
"I KNEW WE HAD ONLY ONE CHANCE..."
THIS HAS TO WORK, OR NOTHING IN TA-METRU WILL BE LEFT STANDING!
SKREE
SKREEE
"I KNEW THE VINE WOULD TRY TO STOP IT. BUT THIS DISK WAS MADE IN KO-METRU. IT HAD THE POWER TO DODGE OBSTACLES!
"AND ENOUGH FREEZE POWER TO STOP EVEN A MORBUZAKH PLANT."
THAT WAS INCREDIBLE! HOW DID YOU KNOW IT WOULD WORK?
I DIDN'T. I TOOK A CHANCE. NOW TELL ME, WHAT WAS A MORBUZAKH VINE DOING THIS FAR INSIDE THE METRU? AND WHY WERE THE VATS MOVING SLOWLY ENOUGH TO BE GRABBED?
I DON'T KNOW ABOUT THE VINES... BUT SOME FOUR-LEGGED CREATURE SABOTAGED THE VAT CONTROLS.
AND JUST WHEN I'M COMING HERE TO FIND NUHRII AND LEARN ABOUT THE GREAT DISK. COINCIDENCE?

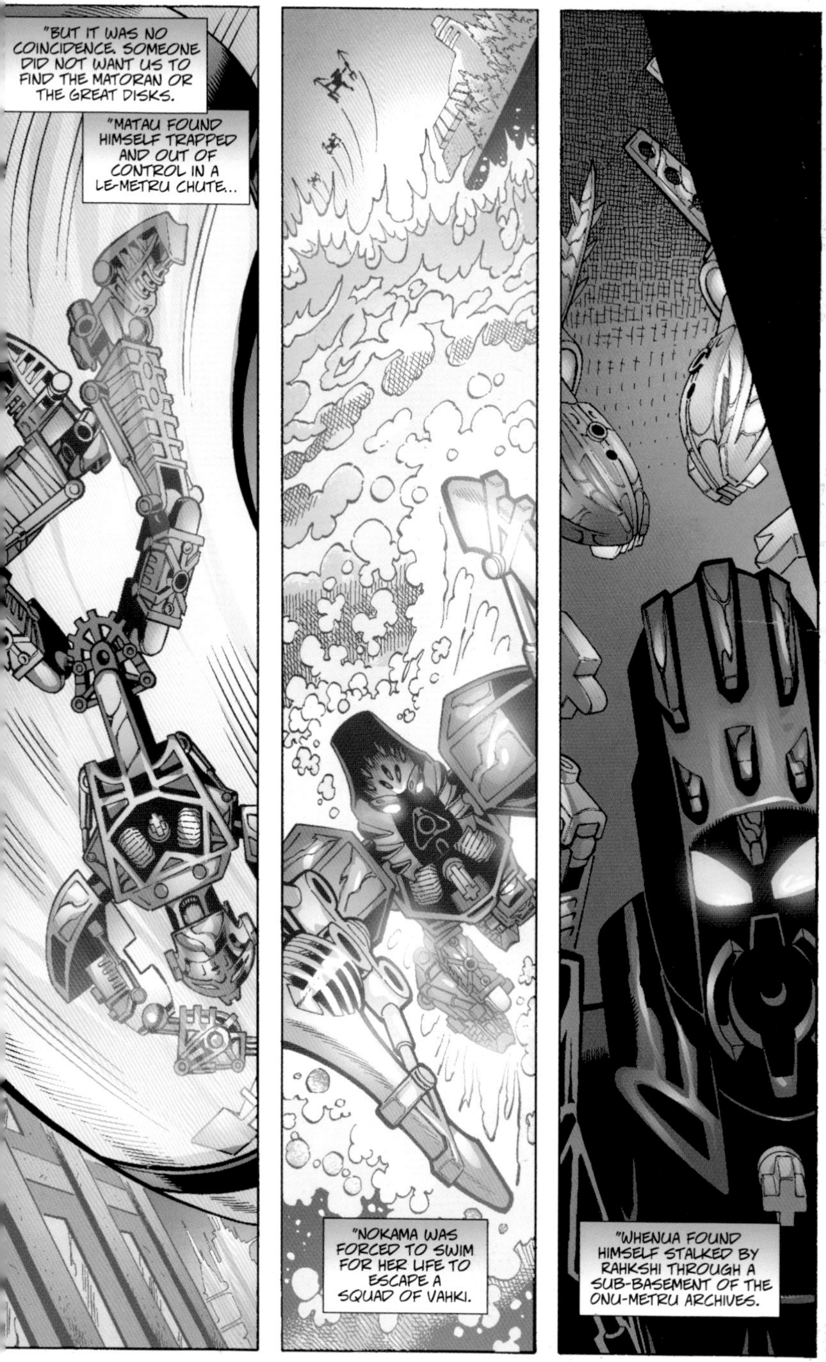
"BUT IT WAS NO COINCIDENCE. SOMEONE DID NOT WANT US TO FIND THE MATORAN OR THE GREAT DISKS.
"MATAU FOUND HIMSELF TRAPPED AND OUT OF CONTROL IN A LE-METRU CHUTE...
"NOKAMA WAS FORCED TO SWIM FOR HER LIFE TO ESCAPE A SQUAD OF VAHKI.
"WHENUA FOUND HIMSELF STALKED BY RAHKSHI THROUGH A SUB-BASEMENT OF THE ONU-METRU ARCHIVES.

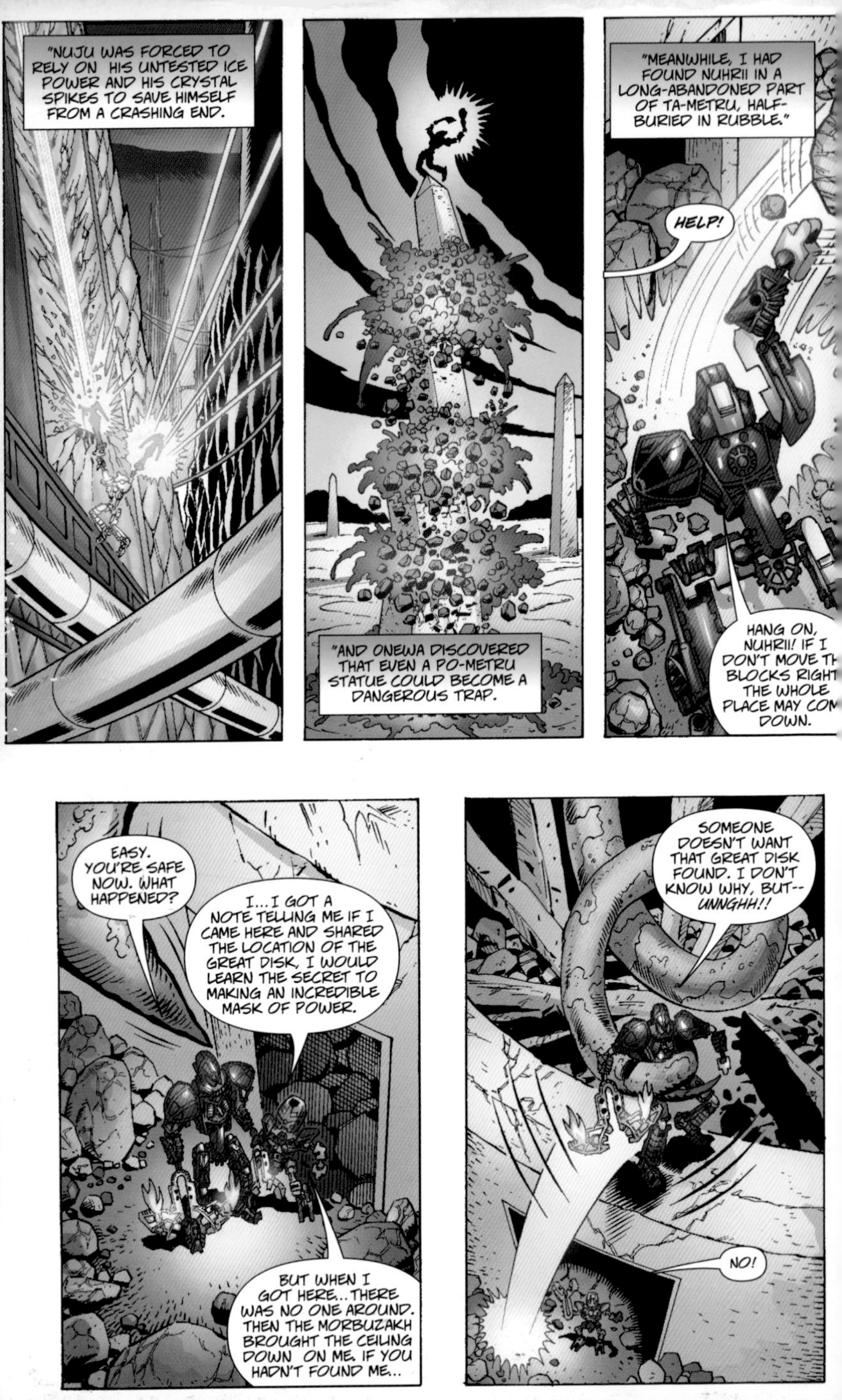
"NUJU WAS FORCED TO RELY ON HIS UNTESTED ICE POWER AND HIS CRYSTAL SPIKES TO SAVE HIMSELF FROM A CRASHING END.
"AND ONEWA DISCOVERED THAT EVEN A PO-METRU STATUE COULD BECOME A DANGEROUS TRAP.
"MEANWHILE, I HAD FOUND NUHRII IN A LONG-ABANDONED PART OF TA-METRU, HALF-BURIED IN RUBBLE."
HELP!
HANG ON, NUHRII! IF I DON'T MOVE TH BLOCKS RIGHT THE WHOLE PLACE MAY COM DOWN.
EASY. YOU'RE SAFE NOW. WHAT HAPPENED?
I... I GOT A NOTE TELLING ME IF I CAME HERE AND SHARED THE LOCATION OF THE GREAT DISK, I WOULD LEARN THE SECRET TO MAKING AN INCREDIBLE MASK OF POWER.
BUT WHEN I GOT HERE... THERE WAS NO ONE AROUND. THEN THE MORBUZAKH BROUGHT THE CEILING DOWN ON ME. IF YOU HADN'T FOUND ME...
SOMEONE DOESN'T WANT THAT GREAT DISK FOUND. I DON'T KNOW WHY, BUT-- UNNGHH!!
NO!

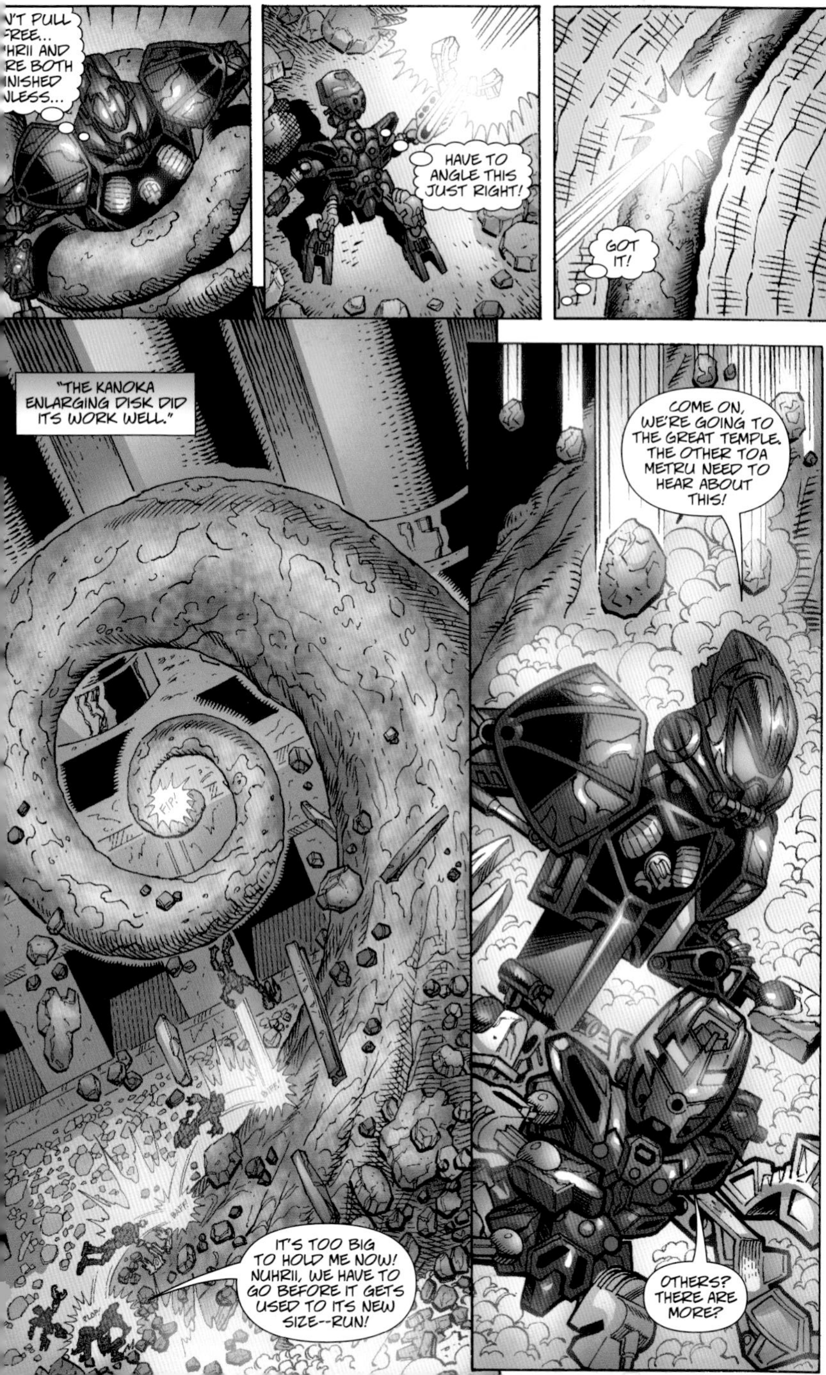

N'T PULL FREE... HRII AND RE BOTH INISHED NLESS...
HAVE TO ANGLE THIS JUST RIGHT!
GOT IT!
"THE KANOKA ENLARGING DISK DID ITS WORK WELL."
FIP!
IT'S TOO BIG TO HOLD ME NOW! NUHRII, WE HAVE TO GO BEFORE IT GETS USED TO ITS NEW SIZE--RUN!
COME ON, WE'RE GOING TO THE GREAT TEMPLE. THE OTHER TOA METRU NEED TO HEAR ABOUT THIS!
OTHERS? THERE ARE MORE?

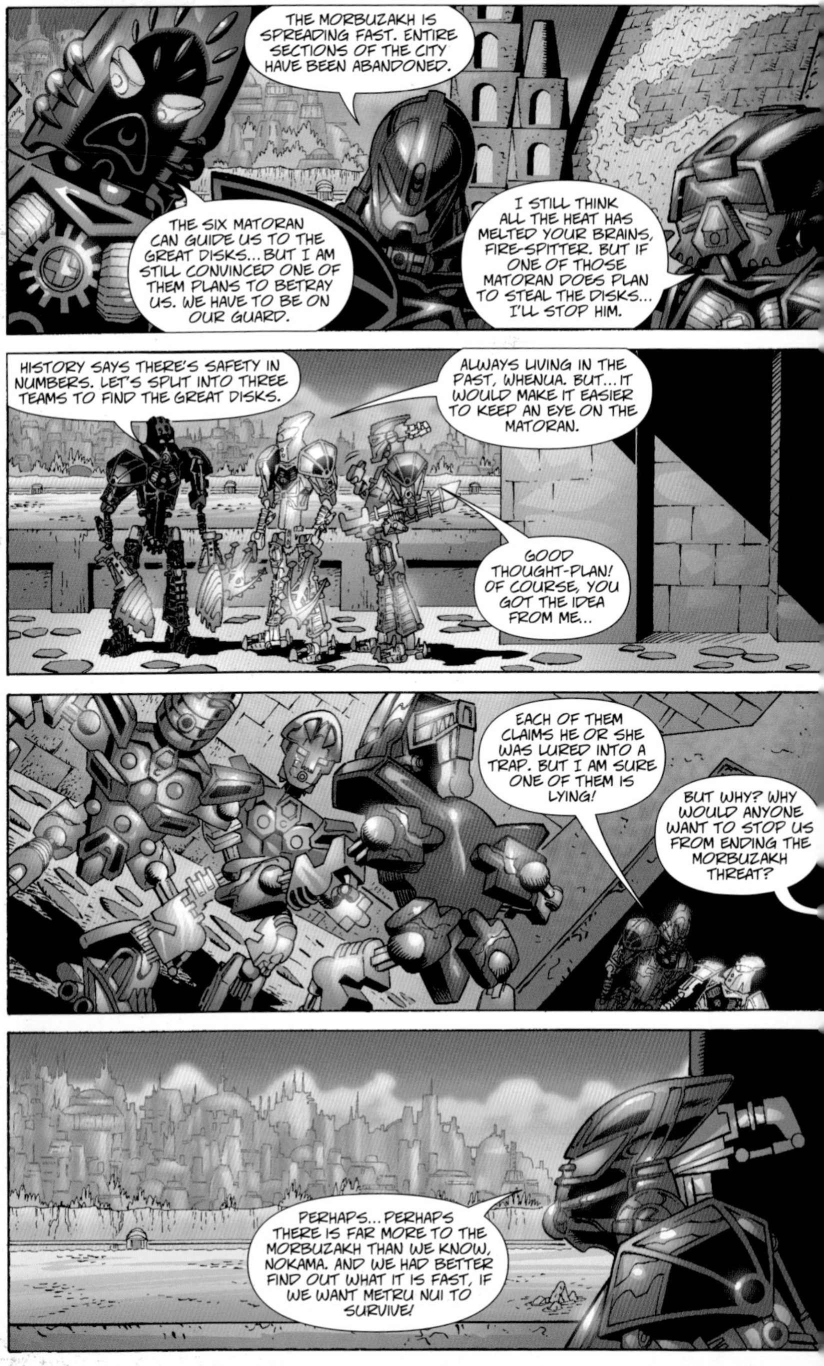

THE MORBUZAKH IS SPREADING FAST. ENTIRE SECTIONS OF THE CITY HAVE BEEN ABANDONED.
THE SIX MATORAN CAN GUIDE US TO THE GREAT DISKS... BUT I AM STILL CONVINCED ONE OF THEM PLANS TO BETRAY US. WE HAVE TO BE ON OUR GUARD.
I STILL THINK ALL THE HEAT HAS MELTED YOUR BRAINS, FIRE-SPITTER. BUT IF ONE OF THOSE MATORAN DOES PLAN TO STEAL THE DISKS... I'LL STOP HIM.
HISTORY SAYS THERE'S SAFETY IN NUMBERS. LET'S SPLIT INTO THREE TEAMS TO FIND THE GREAT DISKS.
ALWAYS LIVING IN THE PAST, WHENUA. BUT... IT WOULD MAKE IT EASIER TO KEEP AN EYE ON THE MATORAN.
GOOD THOUGHT-PLAN! OF COURSE, YOU GOT THE IDEA FROM ME...
EACH OF THEM CLAIMS HE OR SHE WAS LURED INTO A TRAP. BUT I AM SURE ONE OF THEM IS LYING!
BUT WHY? WHY WOULD ANYONE WANT TO STOP US FROM ENDING THE MORBUZAKH THREAT?
PERHAPS... PERHAPS THERE IS FAR MORE TO THE MORBUZAKH THAN WE KNOW, NOKAMA. AND WE HAD BETTER FIND OUT WHAT IT IS FAST, IF WE WANT METRU NUI TO SURVIVE!

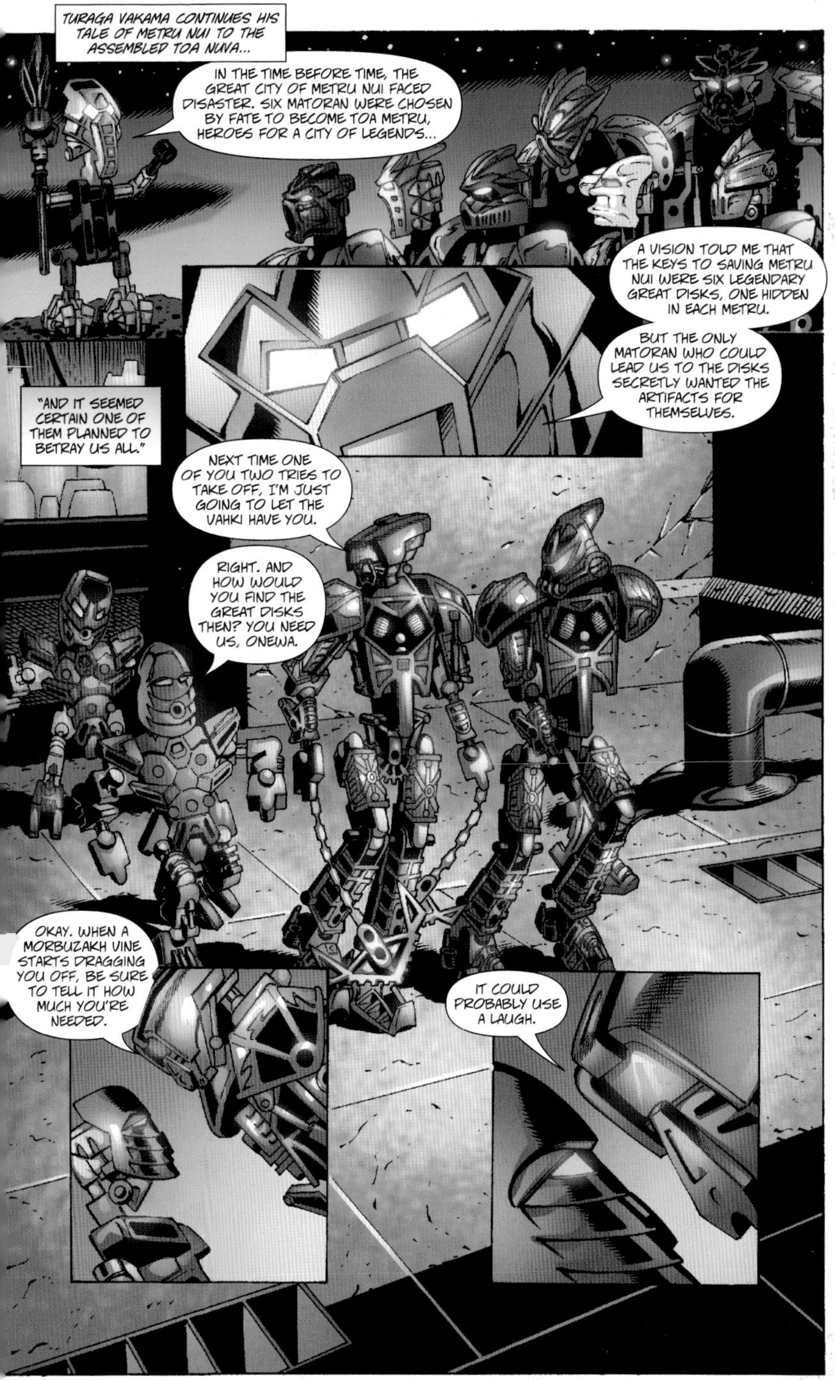
TURAGA VAKAMA CONTINUES HIS TALE OF METRU NUI TO THE ASSEMBLED TOA NUVA...
IN THE TIME BEFORE TIME, THE GREAT CITY OF METRU NUI FACED DISASTER. SIX MATORAN WERE CHOSEN BY FATE TO BECOME TOA METRU, HEROES FOR A CITY OF LEGENDS...
A VISION TOLD ME THAT THE KEYS TO SAVING METRU NUI WERE SIX LEGENDARY GREAT DISKS, ONE HIDDEN IN EACH METRU.
BUT THE ONLY MATORAN WHO COULD LEAD US TO THE DISKS SECRETLY WANTED THE ARTIFACTS FOR THEMSELVES.
"AND IT SEEMED CERTAIN ONE OF THEM PLANNED TO BETRAY US ALL."
NEXT TIME ONE OF YOU TWO TRIES TO TAKE OFF, I'M JUST GOING TO LET THE VAHKI HAVE YOU.
RIGHT. AND HOW WOULD YOU FIND THE GREAT DISKS THEN? YOU NEED US, ONEWA.
OKAY. WHEN A MORBUZAKH VINE STARTS DRAGGING YOU OFF, BE SURE TO TELL IT HOW MUCH YOU'RE NEEDED.
IT COULD PROBABLY USE A LAUGH.

THE VINES! FREE YOURSELF AND GET OUT OF HERE, NUHRII-- GET THE GREAT DISK TO ONEWA!

IT'S TOO STRONG! WE'RE VAHKI BONES!

I NEED YOU TO LOAD MY LAST DISK INTO THE LAUNCHER. IT'S OUR ONLY CHANCE!

VAKAMA, IT'S POWER CODE 4--DO YOU REALIZE WHAT THAT WILL DO? IT MIGHT MAKE THE MORBUZAKH EVEN MORE DANGEROUS!

WE HAVE NO CHOICE! LOAD AND LAUNCH!

NOW!

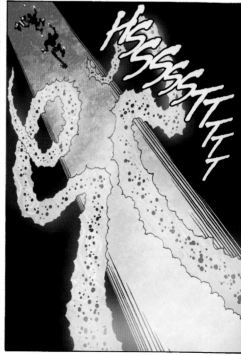

HSSSSTTTT

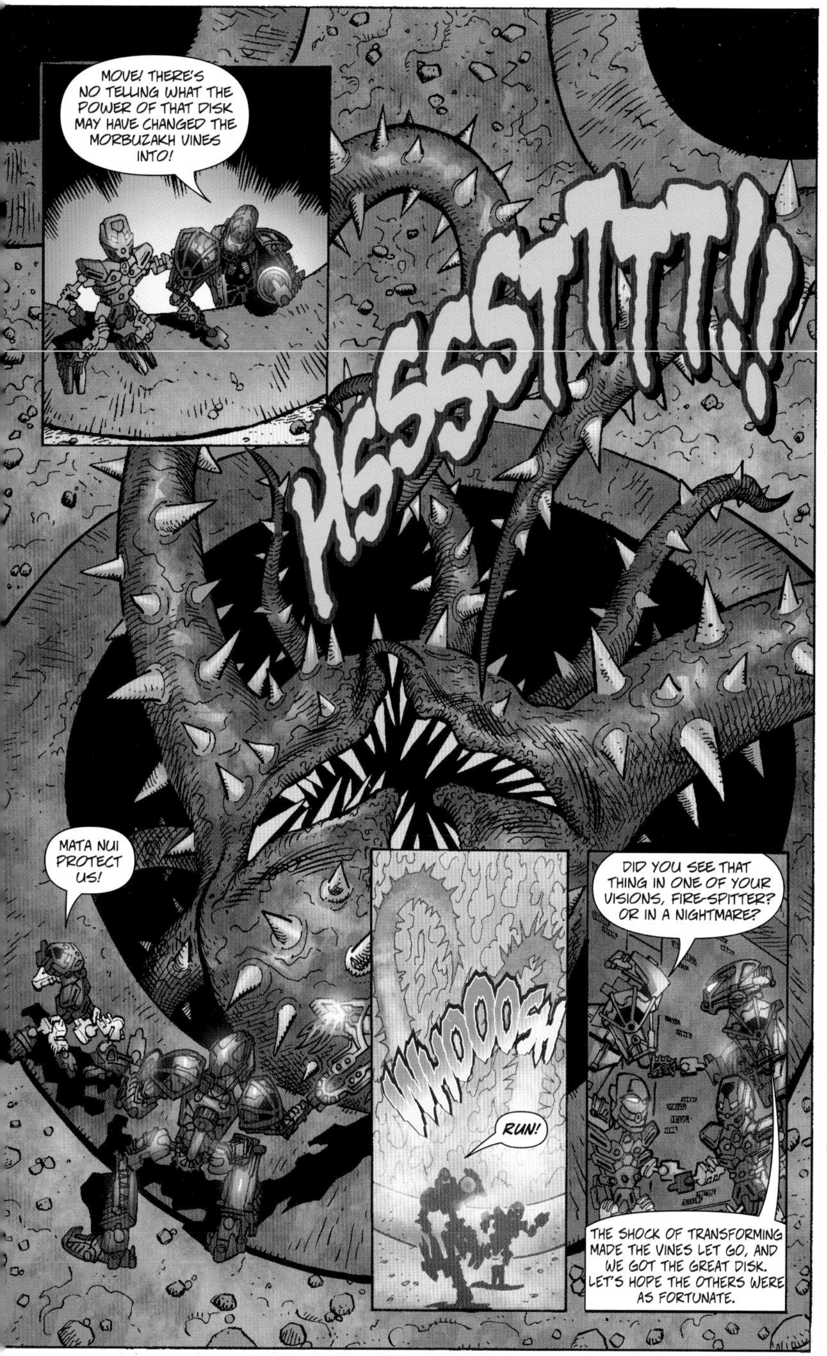
MOVE! THERE'S NO TELLING WHAT THE POWER OF THAT DISK MAY HAVE CHANGED THE MORBUZAKH VINES INTO!
KSSSTTTT!!
MATA NUI PROTECT US!
WHOOOSH
RUN!
DID YOU SEE THAT THING IN ONE OF YOUR VISIONS, FIRE-SPITTER? OR IN A NIGHTMARE?
THE SHOCK OF TRANSFORMING MADE THE VINES LET GO, AND WE GOT THE GREAT DISK. LET'S HOPE THE OTHERS WERE AS FORTUNATE.

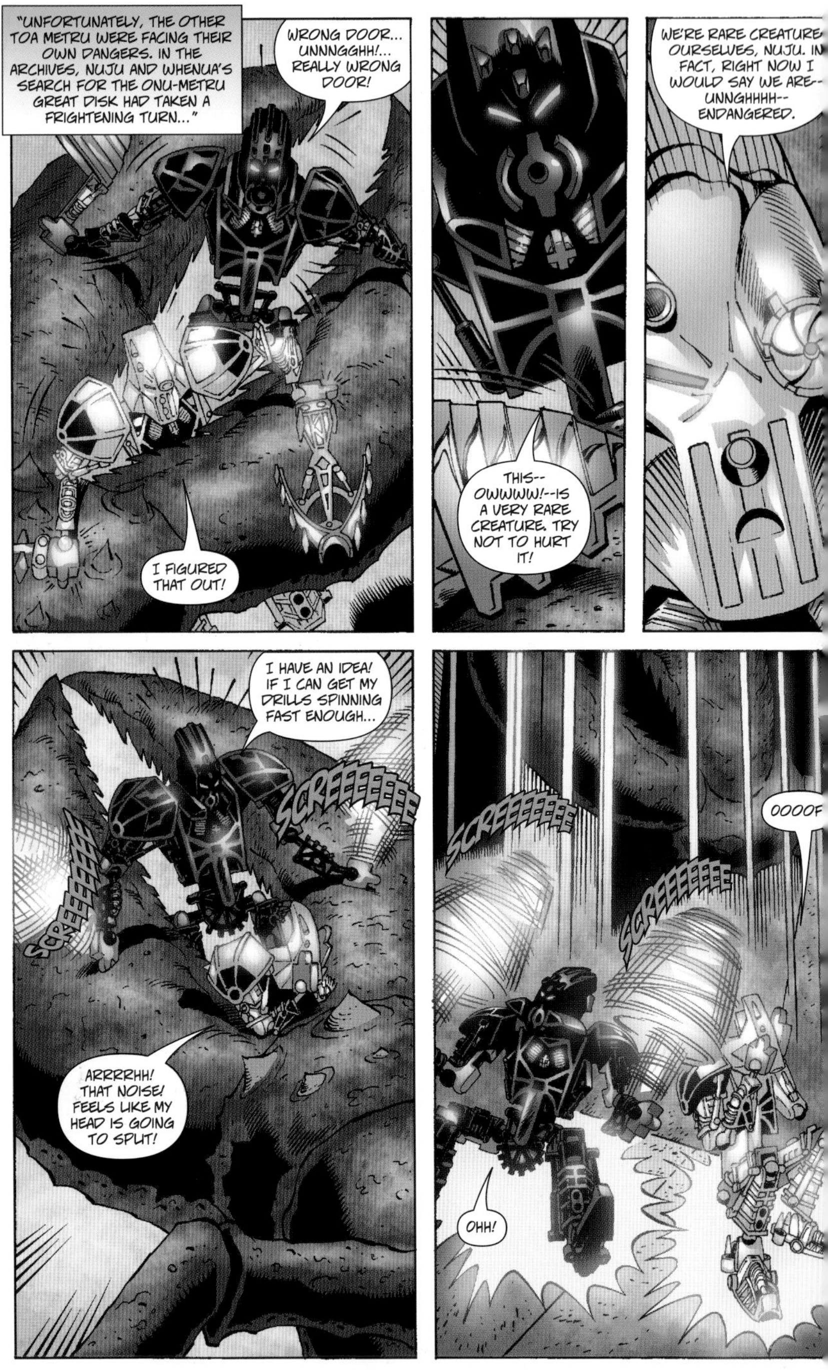
"UNFORTUNATELY, THE OTHER TOA METRU WERE FACING THEIR OWN DANGERS. IN THE ARCHIVES, NUJU AND WHENUA'S SEARCH FOR THE ONU-METRU GREAT DISK HAD TAKEN A FRIGHTENING TURN..."
WRONG DOOR... UNNNGGHH!... REALLY WRONG DOOR!
I FIGURED THAT OUT!
THIS--OWWWW!--IS A VERY RARE CREATURE. TRY NOT TO HURT IT!
WE'RE RARE CREATURE OURSELVES, NUJU. IN FACT, RIGHT NOW I WOULD SAY WE ARE--UNNGHHHH--ENDANGERED.
I HAVE AN IDEA! IF I CAN GET MY DRILLS SPINNING FAST ENOUGH...
SCREEEEEEE
SCREEEEEEE
ARRRRHH! THAT NOISE! FEELS LIKE MY HEAD IS GOING TO SPLIT!
SCREEEEEEE
SCREEEEEEE
OOOOF
OHH!

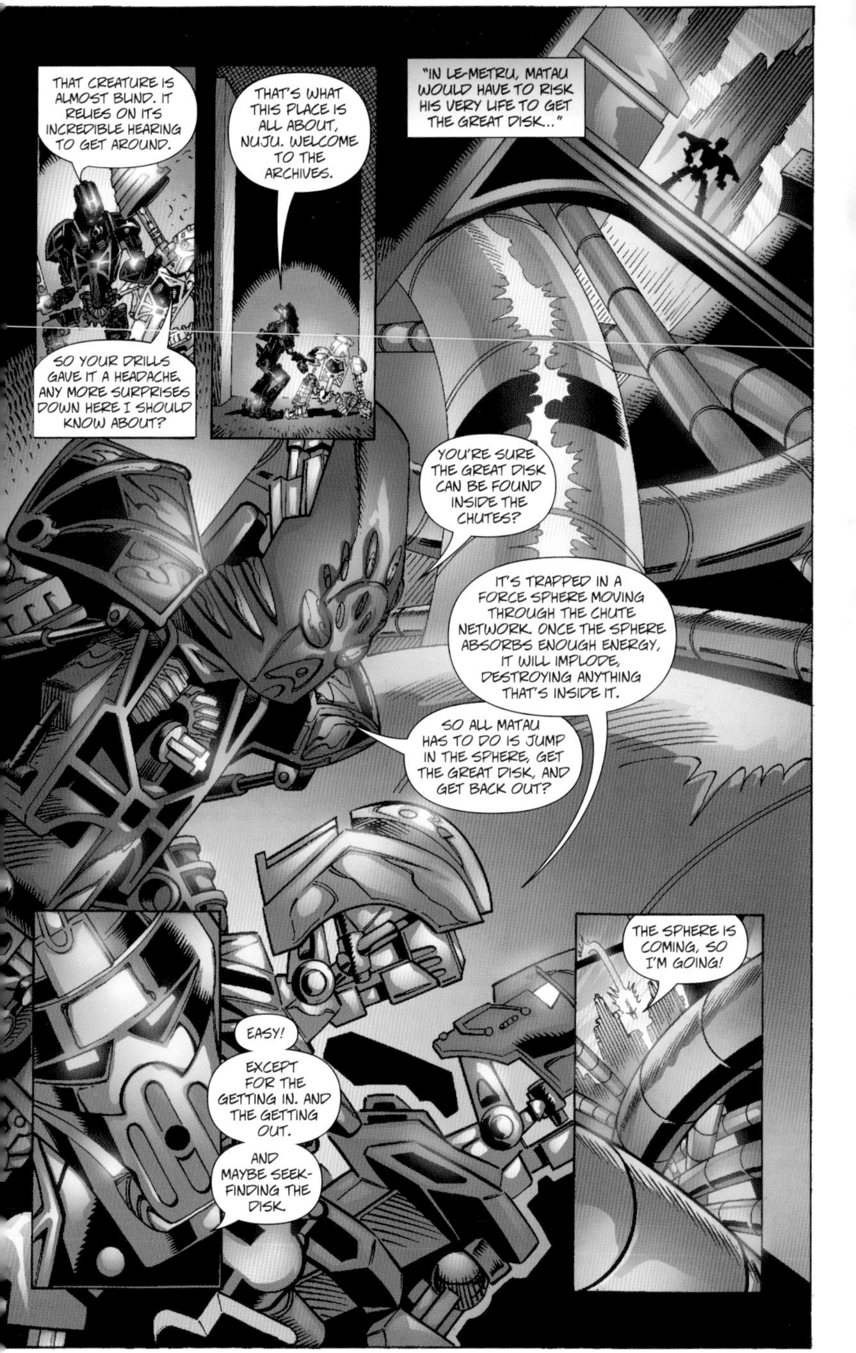
THAT CREATURE IS ALMOST BLIND. IT RELIES ON ITS INCREDIBLE HEARING TO GET AROUND.
SO YOUR DRILLS GAVE IT A HEADACHE. ANY MORE SURPRISES DOWN HERE I SHOULD KNOW ABOUT?
THAT'S WHAT THIS PLACE IS ALL ABOUT, NUJU. WELCOME TO THE ARCHIVES.
"IN LE-METRU, MATAU WOULD HAVE TO RISK HIS VERY LIFE TO GET THE GREAT DISK..."
YOU'RE SURE THE GREAT DISK CAN BE FOUND INSIDE THE CHUTES?
IT'S TRAPPED IN A FORCE SPHERE MOVING THROUGH THE CHUTE NETWORK. ONCE THE SPHERE ABSORBS ENOUGH ENERGY, IT WILL IMPLODE, DESTROYING ANYTHING THAT'S INSIDE IT.
SO ALL MATAU HAS TO DO IS JUMP IN THE SPHERE, GET THE GREAT DISK, AND GET BACK OUT?
EASY!
EXCEPT FOR THE GETTING IN. AND THE GETTING OUT.
AND MAYBE SEEK-FINDING THE DISK.
THE SPHERE IS COMING, SO I'M GOING!

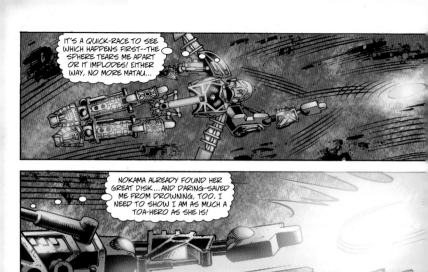

IT'S A QUICK-RACE TO SEE WHICH HAPPENS FIRST--THE SPHERE TEARS ME APART OR IT IMPLODES! EITHER WAY, NO MORE MATAU...

NOKAMA ALREADY FOUND HER GREAT DISK...AND DARING-SAVED ME FROM DROWNING, TOO. I NEED TO SHOW I AM AS MUCH A TOA-HERO AS SHE IS!

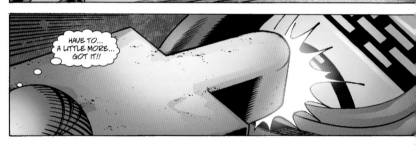

HAVE TO... A LITTLE MORE... GOT IT!!

WHOA! TIME TO LEAVE! BUT THERE'S NO PLACE TO QUICK-JUMP FROM.

HAVE TO USE MY POWER--CREATE AN AIR-STORM INSIDE THIS ENERGY SPHERE--AND TRY TO THROW MYSELF CLEAR!

CAN'T BREATHE... CAN'T... NEED MORE POWER...

FREE! I'M--

NO ONE SAID FREEDOM WOULD BE EASY.

KRRAASSHH!

"AND SO OUR SEARCH CONTINUED. FROM THE SNOW-COVERED KNOWLEDGE TOWERS OF KO-METRU ..."

"TO THE SKIES ABOVE THE PO-METRU SCULPTURE FIELDS."

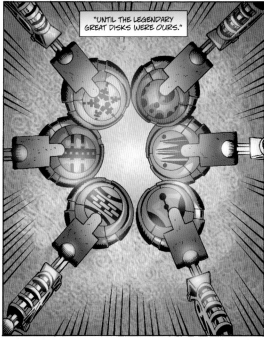

"UNTIL THE LEGENDARY GREAT DISKS WERE OURS."

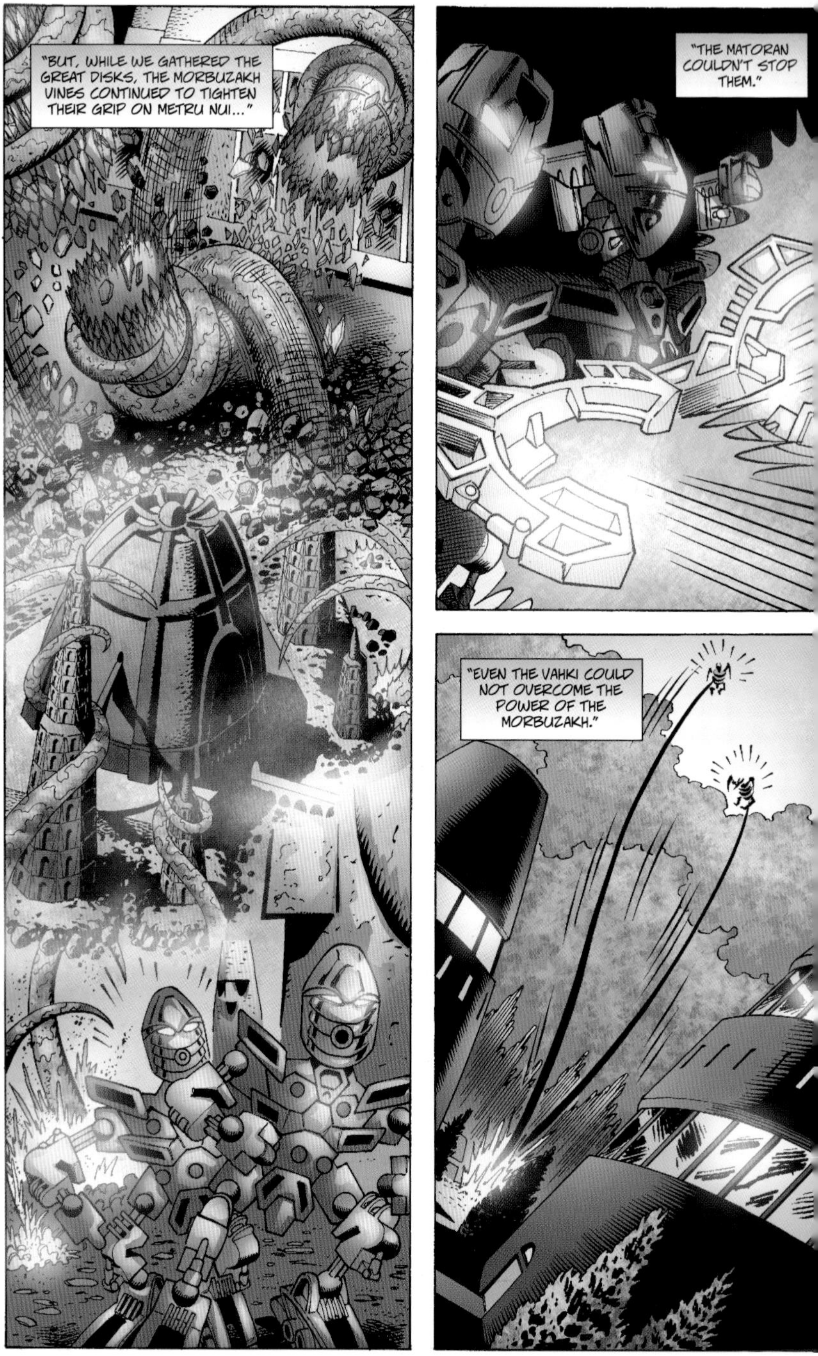
"BUT, WHILE WE GATHERED THE GREAT DISKS, THE MORBUZAKH VINES CONTINUED TO TIGHTEN THEIR GRIP ON METRU NUI..."
"THE MATORAN COULDN'T STOP THEM."
"EVEN THE VAHKI COULD NOT OVERCOME THE POWER OF THE MORBUZAKH."

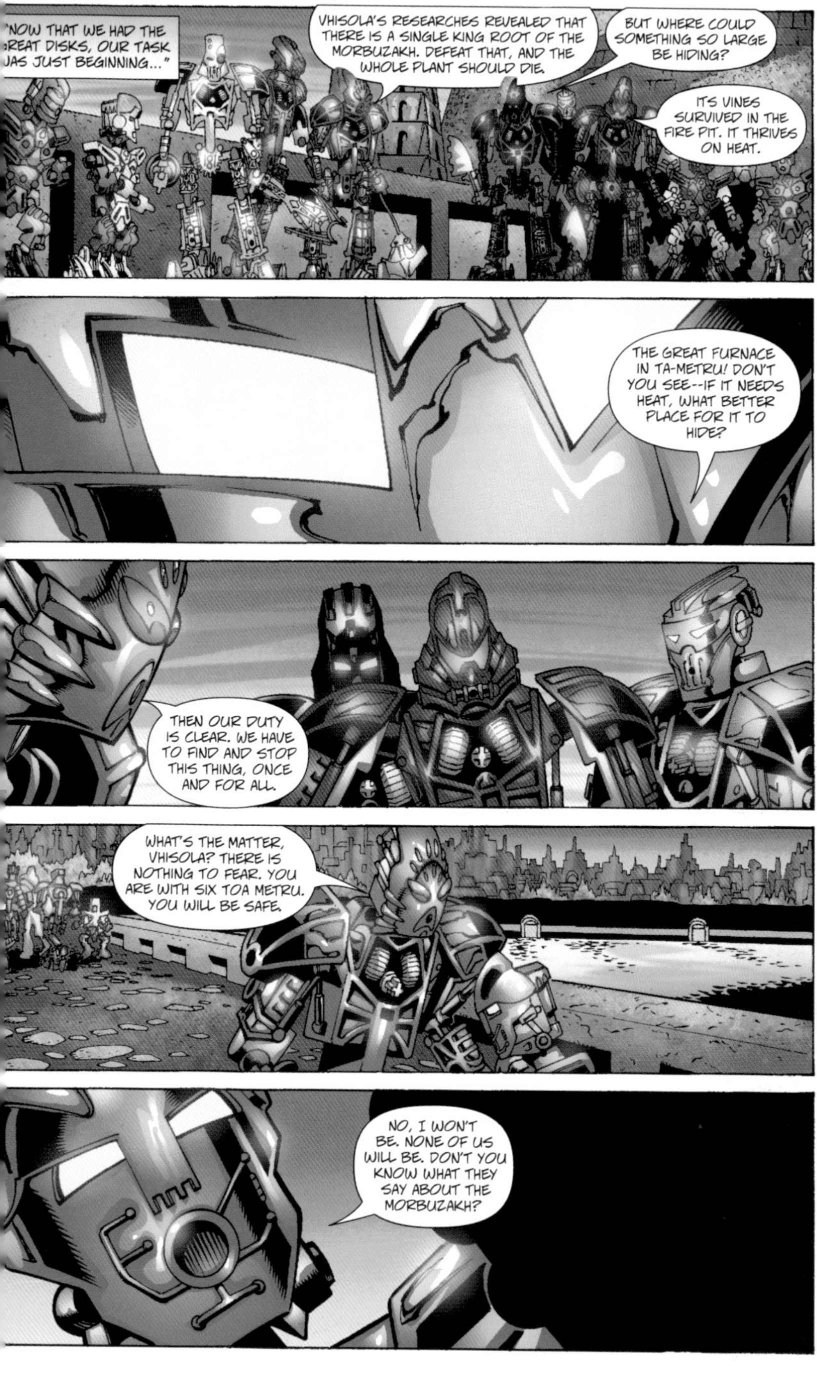

"NOW THAT WE HAD THE GREAT DISKS, OUR TASK WAS JUST BEGINNING..."
VHISOLA'S RESEARCHES REVEALED THAT THERE IS A SINGLE KING ROOT OF THE MORBUZAKH. DEFEAT THAT, AND THE WHOLE PLANT SHOULD DIE.
BUT WHERE COULD SOMETHING SO LARGE BE HIDING?
ITS VINES SURVIVED IN THE FIRE PIT. IT THRIVES ON HEAT.
THE GREAT FURNACE IN TA-METRU! DON'T YOU SEE--IF IT NEEDS HEAT, WHAT BETTER PLACE FOR IT TO HIDE?
THEN OUR DUTY IS CLEAR. WE HAVE TO FIND AND STOP THIS THING, ONCE AND FOR ALL.
WHAT'S THE MATTER, VHISOLA? THERE IS NOTHING TO FEAR. YOU ARE WITH SIX TOA METRU. YOU WILL BE SAFE.
NO, I WON'T BE. NONE OF US WILL BE. DON'T YOU KNOW WHAT THEY SAY ABOUT THE MORBUZAKH?

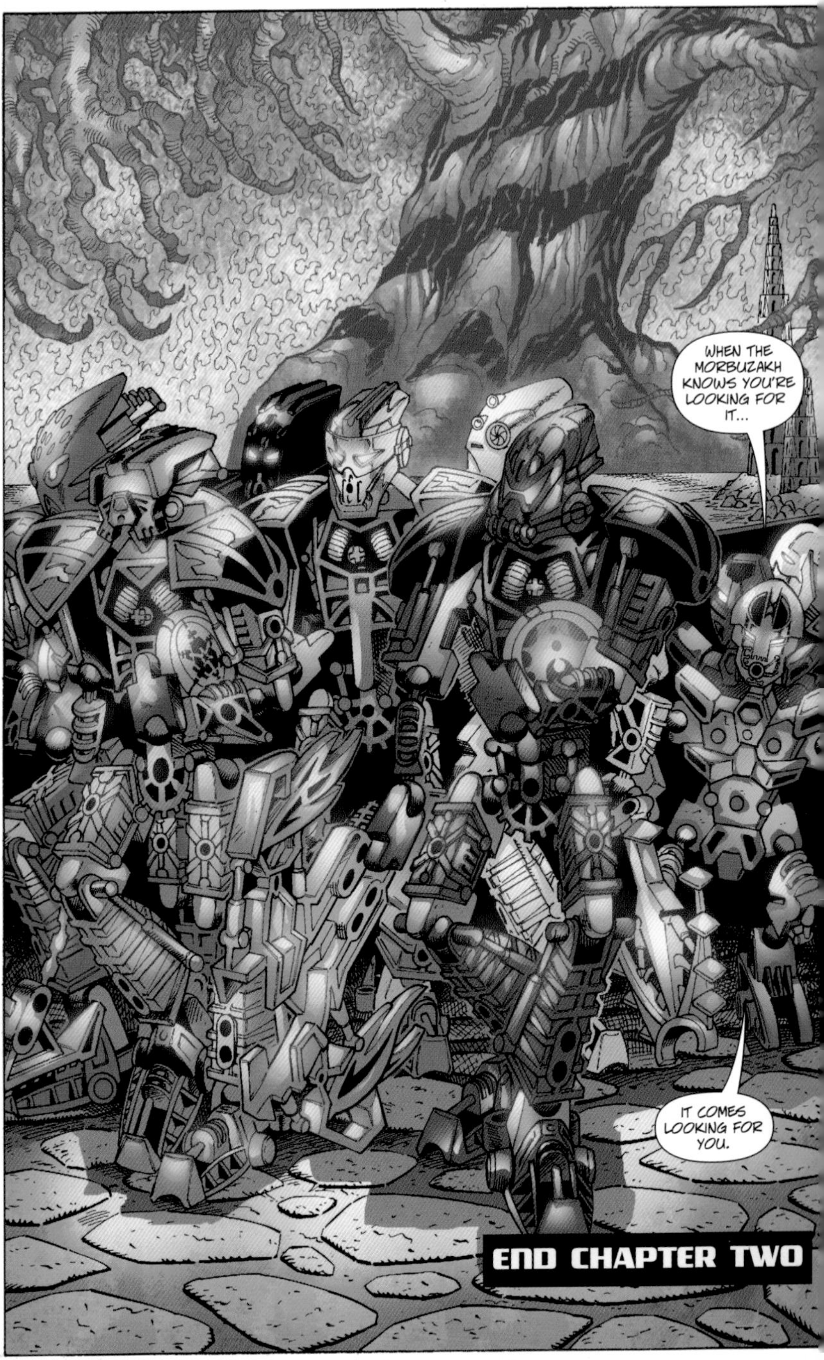
WHEN THE MORBUZAKH KNOWS YOU'RE LOOKING FOR IT...
IT COMES LOOKING FOR YOU.
END CHAPTER TWO

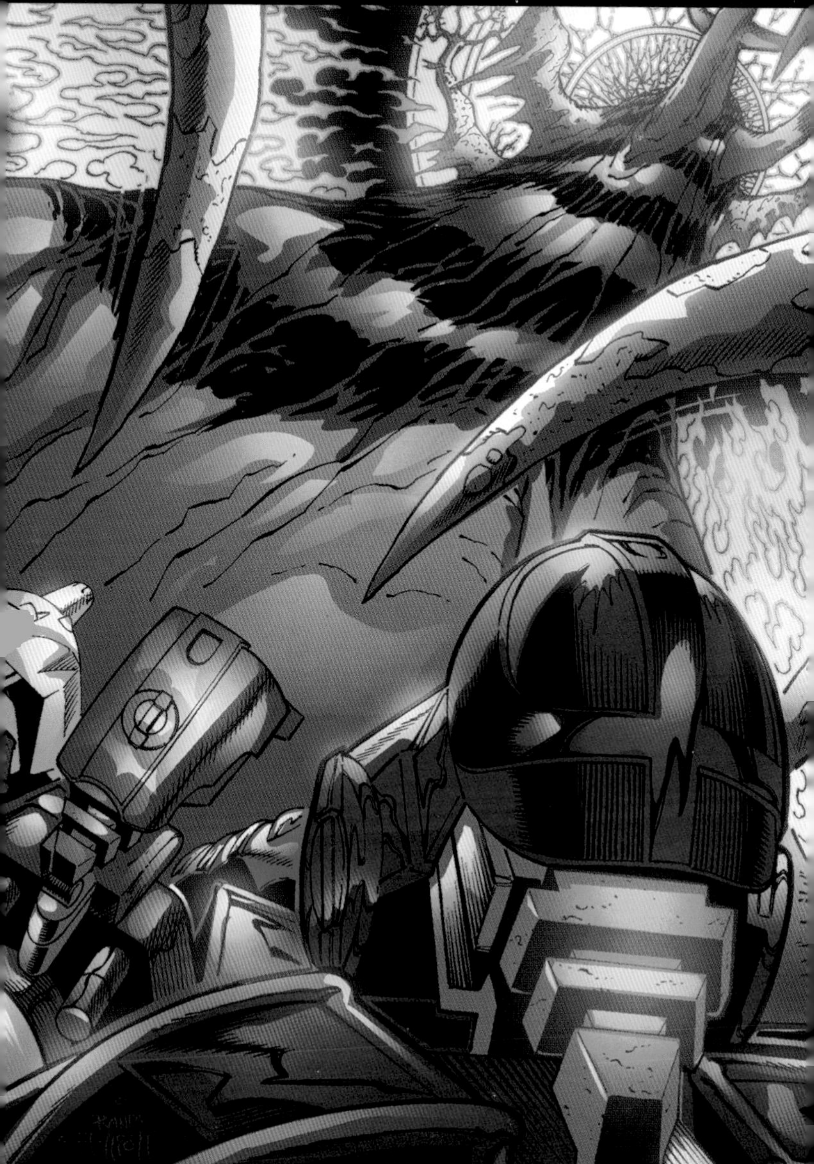

THE VAHKI AR

METRU NUI is confronted by many dangers. Rampaging *MORBUZAKH* vines. *MATORAN* vanishing from their workplaces. Strange beings claiming to be *TOA METRU*. But don't worry, citizen *MATORAN* – the *VAHKI* order enforcement squads are here to keep your city safe. They will watch over you as you work, play, and rest. They will make certain you are always safe, secure and where you are supposed to be. The *VAHKI* will always be nearby to protect you ... whether you like it or not.

Nuurakh

COMMAND CODE: 8614
ZONE OF CONTROL: Ta-Metru
EQUIPMENT: Kanoka disks; Staff of Command, causes target to obey a single command for duration of effect.
ATTRIBUTES: Speed; skill at ambush; resistance to extremes of heat.
PREFERRED TACTIC: Surprise, surround, and capture.

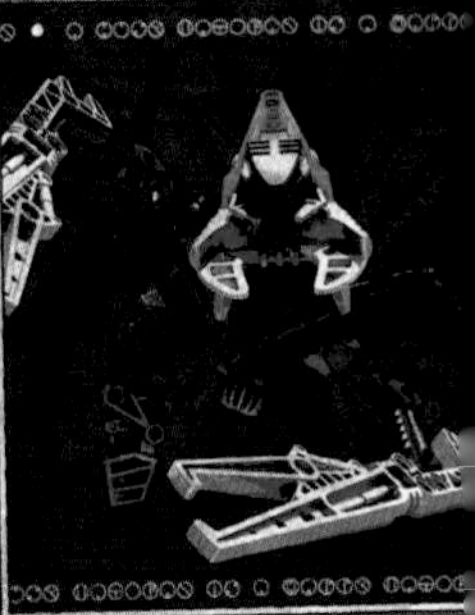

SURRENDER

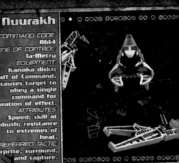

Bordakh

COMMAND CODE: 8615
ZONE OF CONTROL: Ga-Metru
EQUIPMENT: Kanoka disks; Staff of Loyalty, makes target willing to identify any lawbreakers she may observe and summon Vahki for their apprehension.
ATTRIBUTES: Cunning; highly skilled in pursuit; prefer small, mobile groups.
PREFERRED TACTIC: Allow a chase to go on as long as possible before making capture.

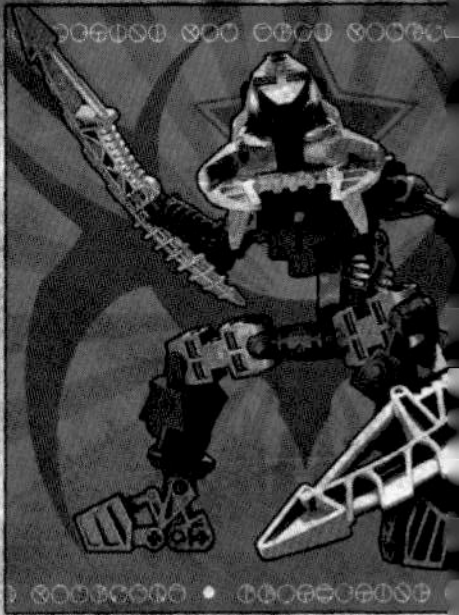

SURRENDER OR

Vorzakh

COMMAND CODE: 8616
ZONE OF CONTROL: Le-Metru
EQUIPMENT: Kanoka disks; Staff of Erasing, temporarily inhibits higher mental functions leaving motor skills only intact.
ATTRIBUTES: Direct; impatient; efficient.
PREFERRED TACTIC: Smash anything standing between it and capture of

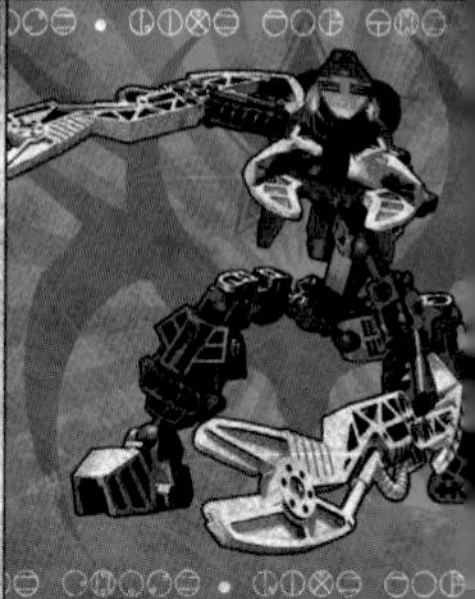

COMING!!!!

Zadakh

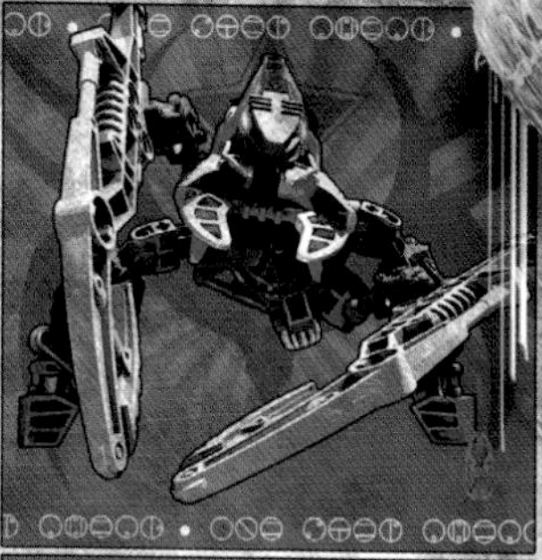
SURRENDER OR RUN

COMMAND CODE: **8617**
ZONE OF CONTROL: **Po-Metru**
EQUIPMENT: **Kanoka disks; Staff of Suggestion, causes target to be extremely susceptible to suggestion for duration of effect.**
ATTRIBUTES: **Unstoppable charge; quick to fight; great strength.**
PREFERRED TACTIC: **Pacify with excessive force.**

Rorzakh

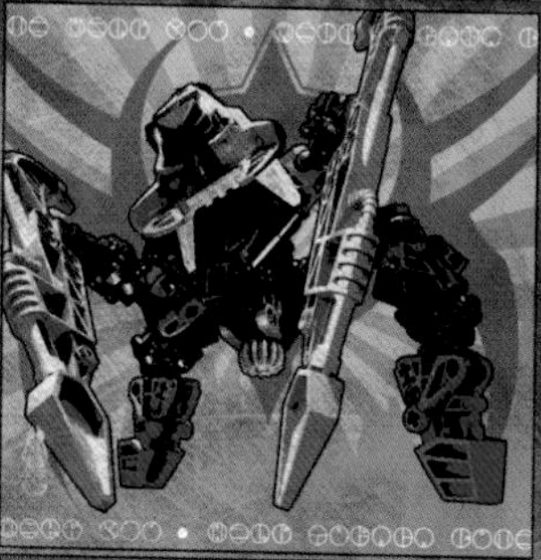
SURRENDER OR RUN

COMMAND CODE: **8618**
ZONE OF CONTROL: **Onu-Metru**
EQUIPMENT: **Kanoka disks; Staff of Presence, Vahki receives audio and visual input from target for duration of effect, without target being aware.**
ATTRIBUTES: **Relentless, fearless.**
PREFERRED TACTIC: **Pursue anywhere, for any length of time, no matter the danger.**

Keerakh

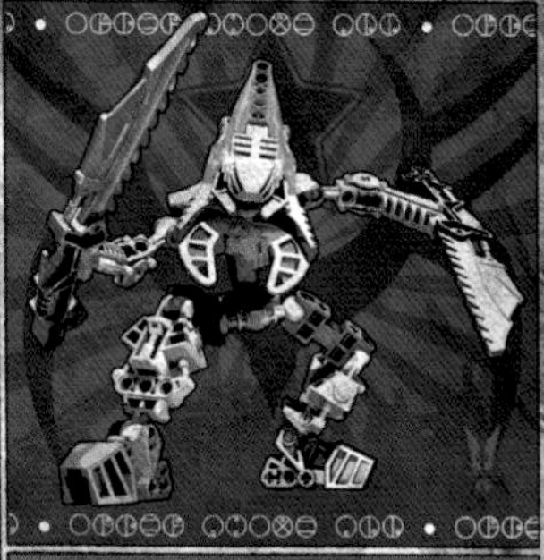
SURRENDER OR RUN

COMMAND CODE: **8619**
ZONE OF CONTROL: **Ko-Metru**
EQUIPMENT: **Kanoka disks; Staff of Confusion, temporarily distorts target's sense of time and place.**
ATTRIBUTES: **Masters of strategy and tactics.**
PREFERRED TACTIC: **Determine where a fleeing target is going and get there first.**

...ordakh

...MAND CODE: 8615
...OF CONTROL: Ga-Metru
EQUIPMENT: Kanoka disks; ...taff of Loyalty, makes target ...illing to identify any lawbreakers she may observe ...nd summon Vahki for their apprehension.
ATTRIBUTES: Cunning; highly skilled in ...; prefer small mobile group...
PREFERRED TA...: Allow a chase to go on as long as possible before making capture.

Vorzak...

COMMAND CO...
ZONE OF CONTR...: Le-Metru
EQUIPMENT: Kanoka disks; ... of ...; temporarily inhibits higher mental functions leaving motor skills only intact.
ATTRIBUTES: Direct; impatient; efficient.
PREFERRED TACTIC: Smash anything standing between it and capture of target.

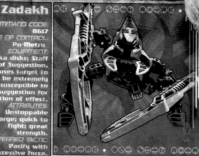

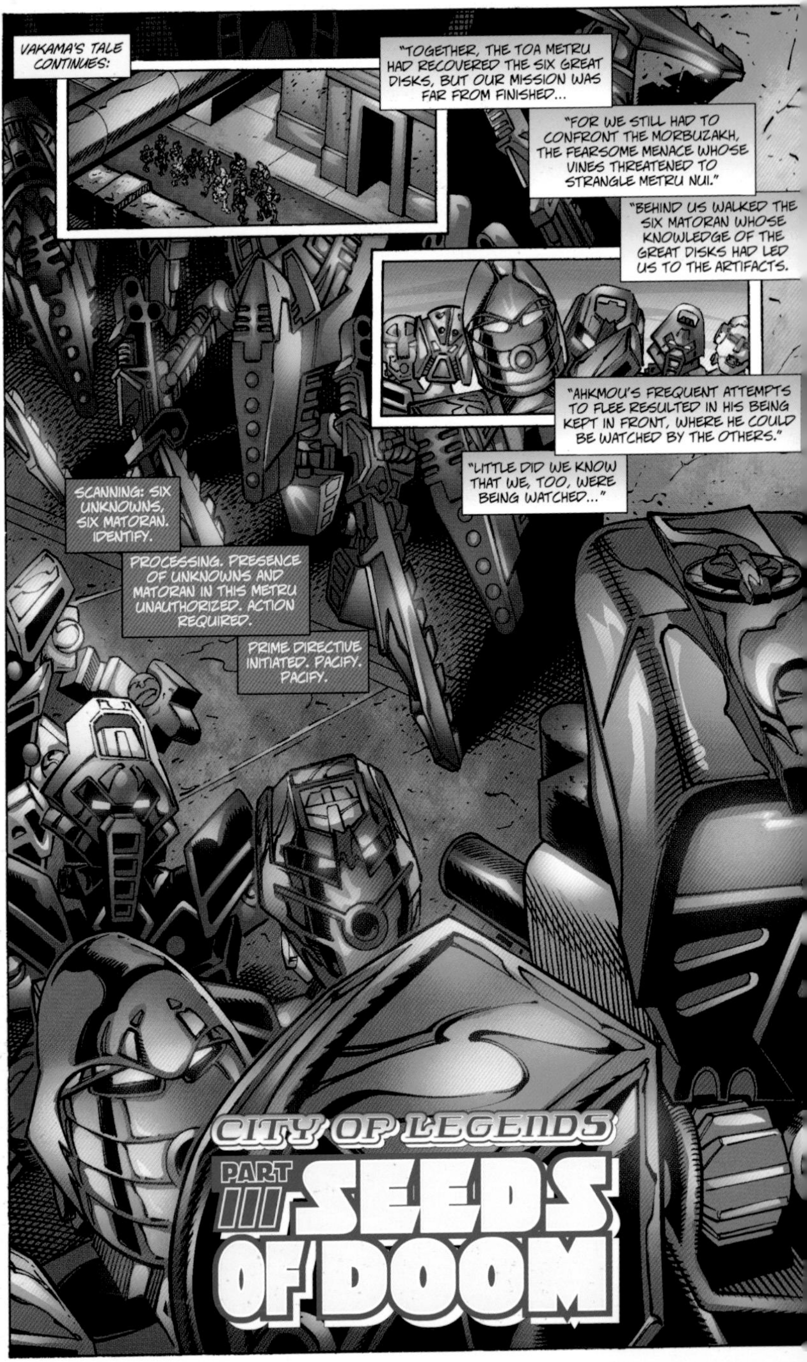

VAKAMA'S TALE CONTINUES:
"TOGETHER, THE TOA METRU HAD RECOVERED THE SIX GREAT DISKS, BUT OUR MISSION WAS FAR FROM FINISHED...
"FOR WE STILL HAD TO CONFRONT THE MORBUZAKH, THE FEARSOME MENACE WHOSE VINES THREATENED TO STRANGLE METRU NUI."
"BEHIND US WALKED THE SIX MATORAN WHOSE KNOWLEDGE OF THE GREAT DISKS HAD LED US TO THE ARTIFACTS.
"AHKMOU'S FREQUENT ATTEMPTS TO FLEE RESULTED IN HIS BEING KEPT IN FRONT, WHERE HE COULD BE WATCHED BY THE OTHERS."
"LITTLE DID WE KNOW THAT WE, TOO, WERE BEING WATCHED..."
SCANNING: SIX UNKNOWNS, SIX MATORAN. IDENTIFY.
PROCESSING. PRESENCE OF UNKNOWNS AND MATORAN IN THIS METRU UNAUTHORIZED. ACTION REQUIRED.
PRIME DIRECTIVE INITIATED. PACIFY. PACIFY. PACIFY.
CITY OF LEGENDS
PART III
SEEDS OF DOOM

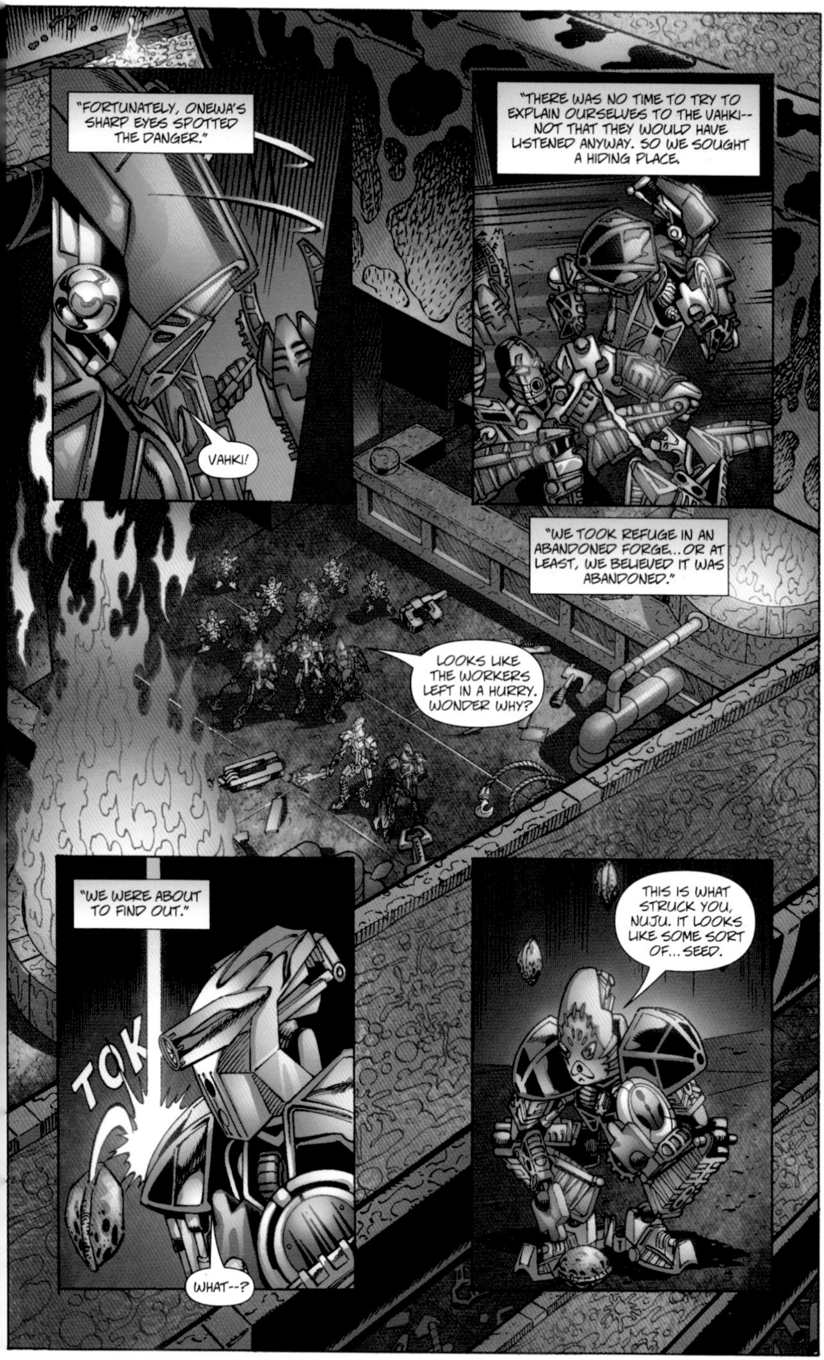
"FORTUNATELY, ONEWA'S SHARP EYES SPOTTED THE DANGER."
VAHKI!
"THERE WAS NO TIME TO TRY TO EXPLAIN OURSELVES TO THE VAHKI-- NOT THAT THEY WOULD HAVE LISTENED ANYWAY. SO WE SOUGHT A HIDING PLACE.
"WE TOOK REFUGE IN AN ABANDONED FORGE...OR AT LEAST, WE BELIEVED IT WAS ABANDONED."
LOOKS LIKE THE WORKERS LEFT IN A HURRY. WONDER WHY?
"WE WERE ABOUT TO FIND OUT."
TOK
WHAT--?
THIS IS WHAT STRUCK YOU, NUJU. IT LOOKS LIKE SOME SORT OF... SEED.

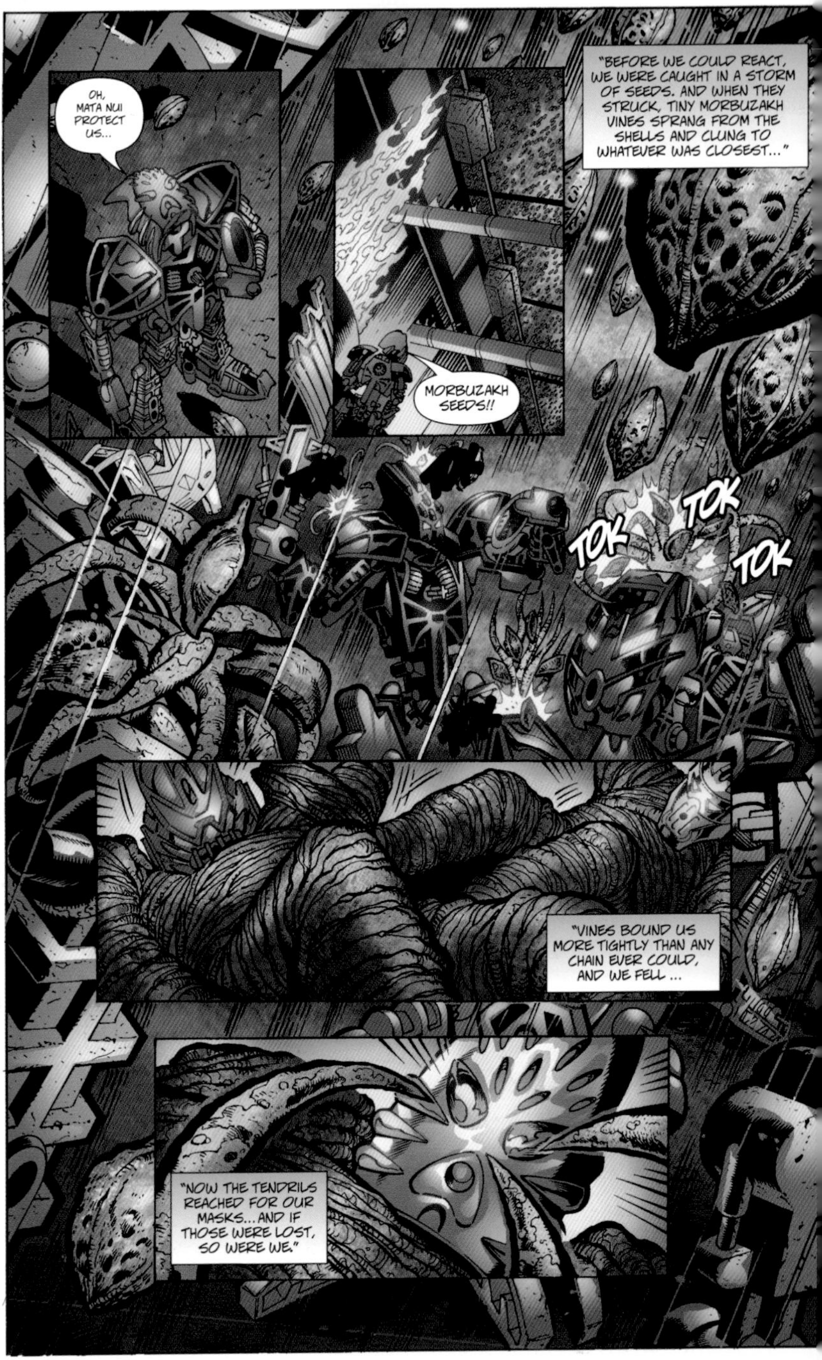

OH, MATA NUI PROTECT US...
MORBUZAKH SEEDS!!
"BEFORE WE COULD REACT, WE WERE CAUGHT IN A STORM OF SEEDS. AND WHEN THEY STRUCK, TINY MORBUZAKH VINES SPRANG FROM THE SHELLS AND CLUNG TO WHATEVER WAS CLOSEST..."
TOK
TOK
TOK
"VINES BOUND US MORE TIGHTLY THAN ANY CHAIN EVER COULD, AND WE FELL ...
"NOW THE TENDRILS REACHED FOR OUR MASKS... AND IF THOSE WERE LOST, SO WERE WE."

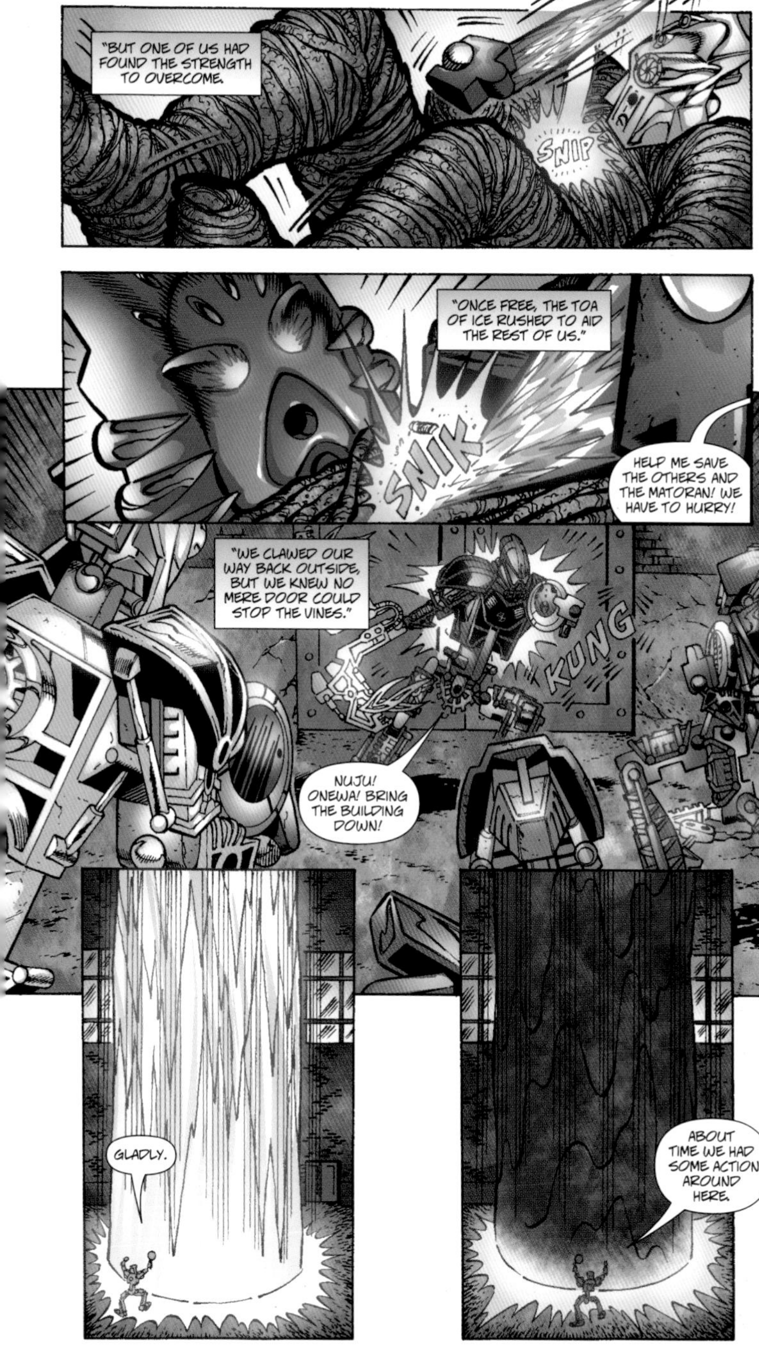
"BUT ONE OF US HAD FOUND THE STRENGTH TO OVERCOME.
SNIP
"ONCE FREE, THE TOA OF ICE RUSHED TO AID THE REST OF US."
SNIK
HELP ME SAVE THE OTHERS AND THE MATORAN! WE HAVE TO HURRY!
"WE CLAWED OUR WAY BACK OUTSIDE, BUT WE KNEW NO MERE DOOR COULD STOP THE VINES."
KUNG
NUJU! ONEWA! BRING THE BUILDING DOWN!
GLADLY.
ABOUT TIME WE HAD SOME ACTION AROUND HERE.

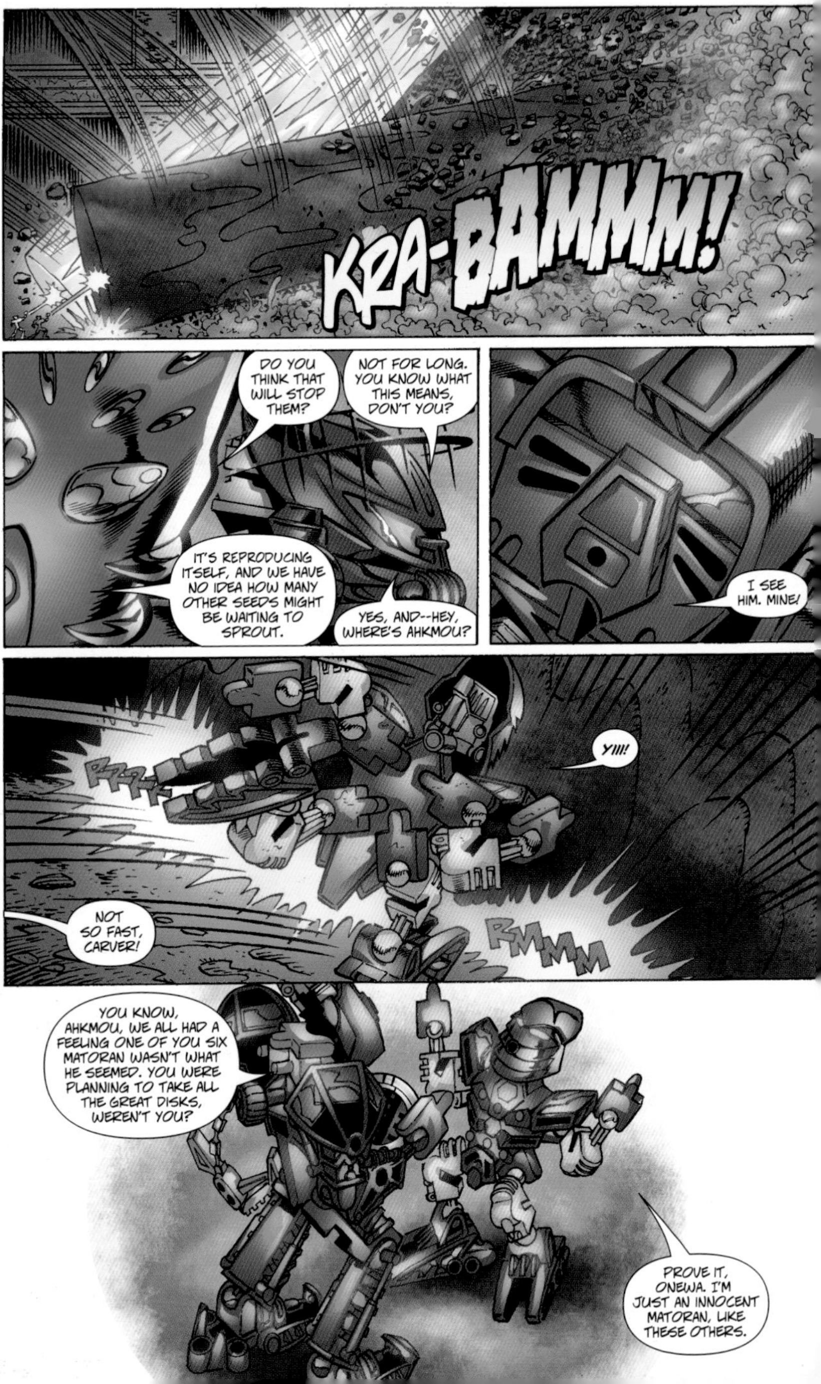
KRA-BAMMM!
DO YOU THINK THAT WILL STOP THEM?
NOT FOR LONG. YOU KNOW WHAT THIS MEANS, DON'T YOU?
IT'S REPRODUCING ITSELF, AND WE HAVE NO IDEA HOW MANY OTHER SEEDS MIGHT BE WAITING TO SPROUT.
YES, AND--HEY, WHERE'S AHKMOU?
I SEE HIM. MINE!
YIII!
NOT SO FAST, CARVER!
RMMMM
YOU KNOW, AHKMOU, WE ALL HAD A FEELING ONE OF YOU SIX MATORAN WASN'T WHAT HE SEEMED. YOU WERE PLANNING TO TAKE ALL THE GREAT DISKS, WEREN'T YOU?
PROVE IT, ONEWA. I'M JUST AN INNOCENT MATORAN, LIKE THESE OTHERS.

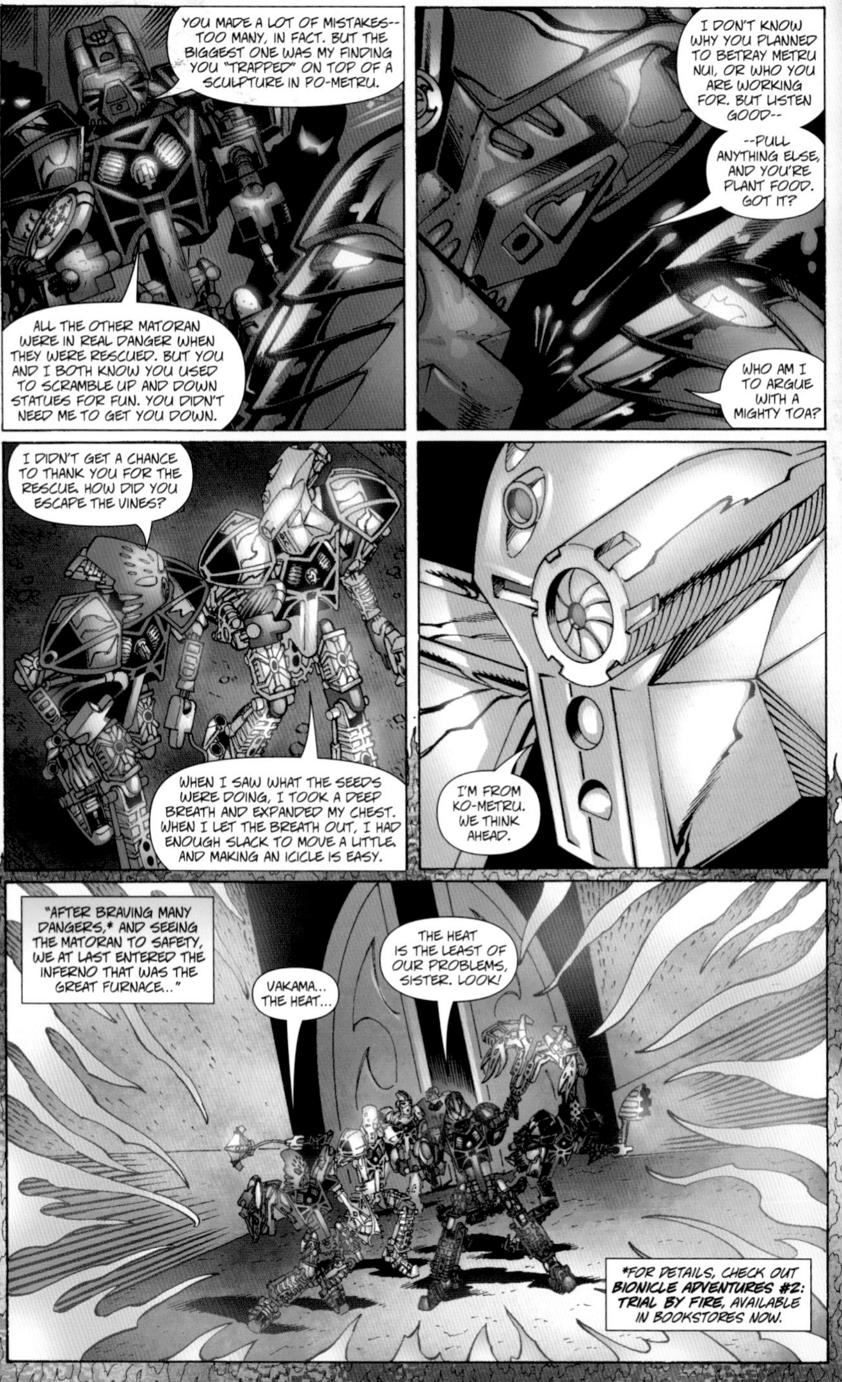
YOU MADE A LOT OF MISTAKES--TOO MANY, IN FACT. BUT THE BIGGEST ONE WAS MY FINDING YOU "TRAPPED" ON TOP OF A SCULPTURE IN PO-METRU.
ALL THE OTHER MATORAN WERE IN REAL DANGER WHEN THEY WERE RESCUED. BUT YOU AND I BOTH KNOW YOU USED TO SCRAMBLE UP AND DOWN STATUES FOR FUN. YOU DIDN'T NEED ME TO GET YOU DOWN.
I DON'T KNOW WHY YOU PLANNED TO BETRAY METRU NUI, OR WHO YOU ARE WORKING FOR. BUT LISTEN GOOD--
--PULL ANYTHING ELSE, AND YOU'RE PLANT FOOD. GOT IT?
WHO AM I TO ARGUE WITH A MIGHTY TOA?
I DIDN'T GET A CHANCE TO THANK YOU FOR THE RESCUE. HOW DID YOU ESCAPE THE VINES?
WHEN I SAW WHAT THE SEEDS WERE DOING, I TOOK A DEEP BREATH AND EXPANDED MY CHEST. WHEN I LET THE BREATH OUT, I HAD ENOUGH SLACK TO MOVE A LITTLE. AND MAKING AN ICICLE IS EASY.
I'M FROM KO-METRU. WE THINK AHEAD.
"AFTER BRAVING MANY DANGERS,* AND SEEING THE MATORAN TO SAFETY, WE AT LAST ENTERED THE INFERNO THAT WAS THE GREAT FURNACE..."
VAKAMA... THE HEAT...
THE HEAT IS THE LEAST OF OUR PROBLEMS, SISTER. LOOK!
*FOR DETAILS, CHECK OUT BIONICLE ADVENTURES #2: TRIAL BY FIRE, AVAILABLE IN BOOKSTORES NOW.

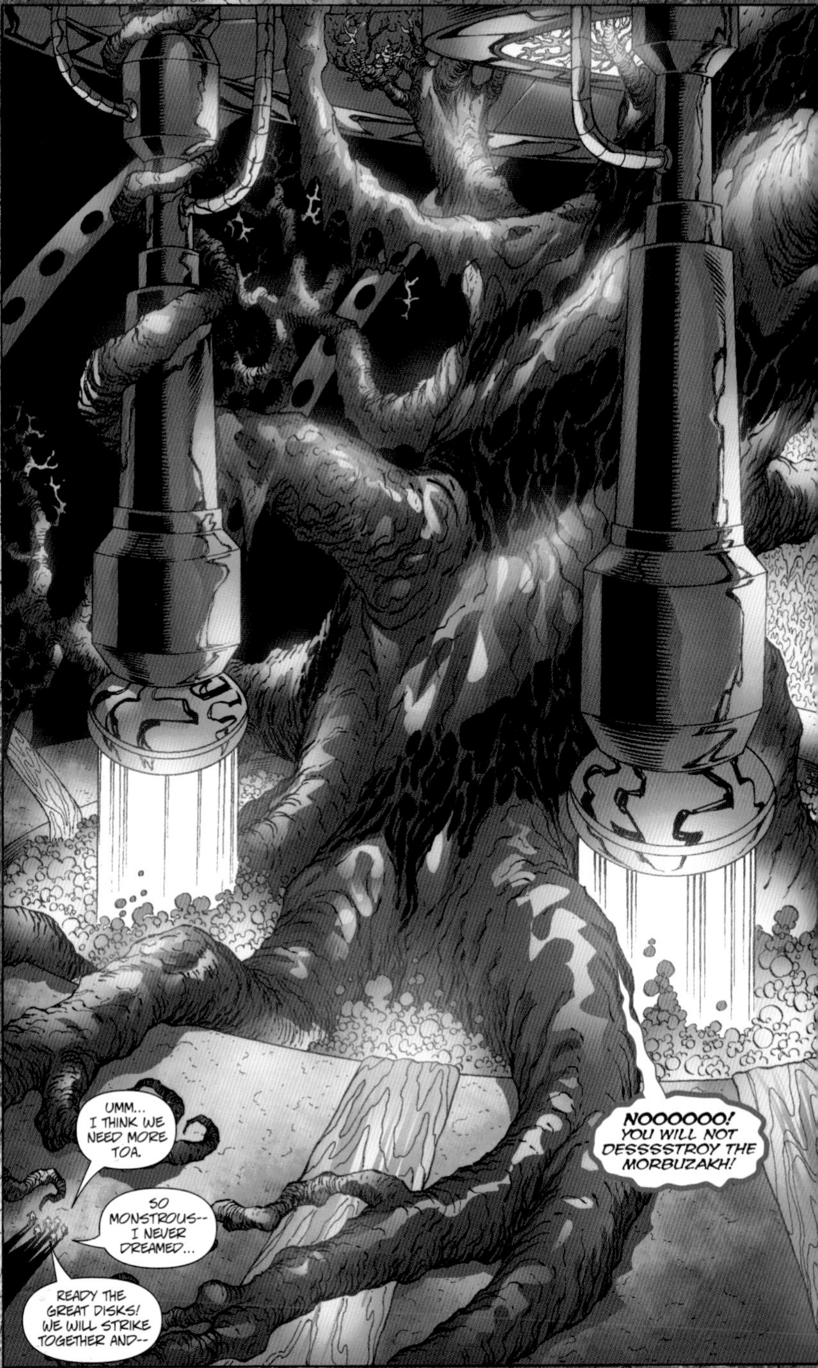

UMM... I THINK WE NEED MORE TOA.
NOOOOOO! YOU WILL NOT DESSSSTROY THE MORBUZAKH!
SO MONSTROUS-- I NEVER DREAMED...
READY THE GREAT DISKS! WE WILL STRIKE TOGETHER AND--

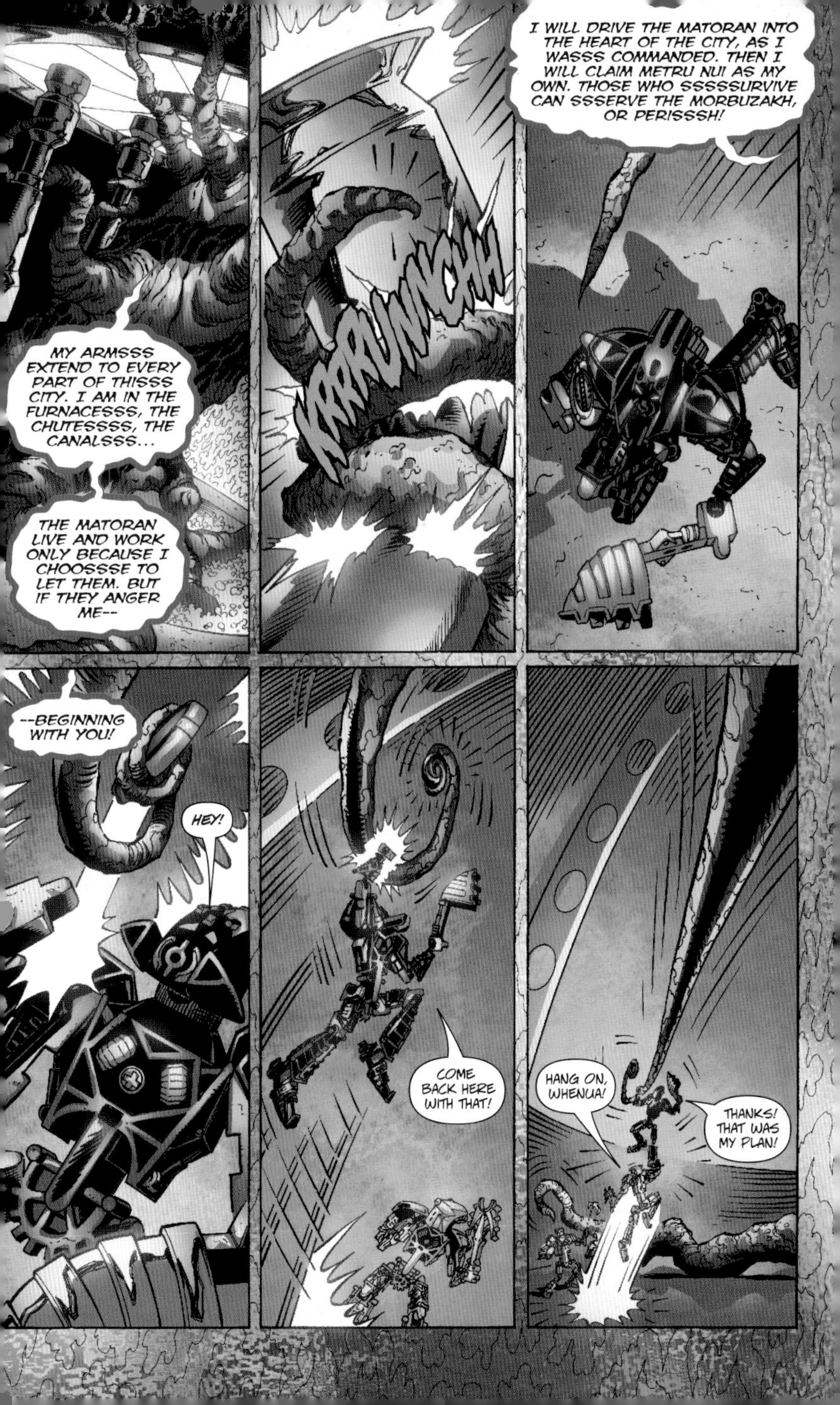

MY ARMSSS EXTEND TO EVERY PART OF THISSS CITY. I AM IN THE FURNACESSS, THE CHUTESSSS, THE CANALSSS...
THE MATORAN LIVE AND WORK ONLY BECAUSE I CHOOSSSE TO LET THEM. BUT IF THEY ANGER ME--
KRRRUNNCHH
I WILL DRIVE THE MATORAN INTO THE HEART OF THE CITY, AS I WASSS COMMANDED. THEN I WILL CLAIM METRU NUI AS MY OWN. THOSE WHO SSSSSURVIVE CAN SSSERVE THE MORBUZAKH, OR PERISSSH!
--BEGINNING WITH YOU!
HEY!
COME BACK HERE WITH THAT!
HANG ON, WHENUA!
THANKS! THAT WAS MY PLAN!

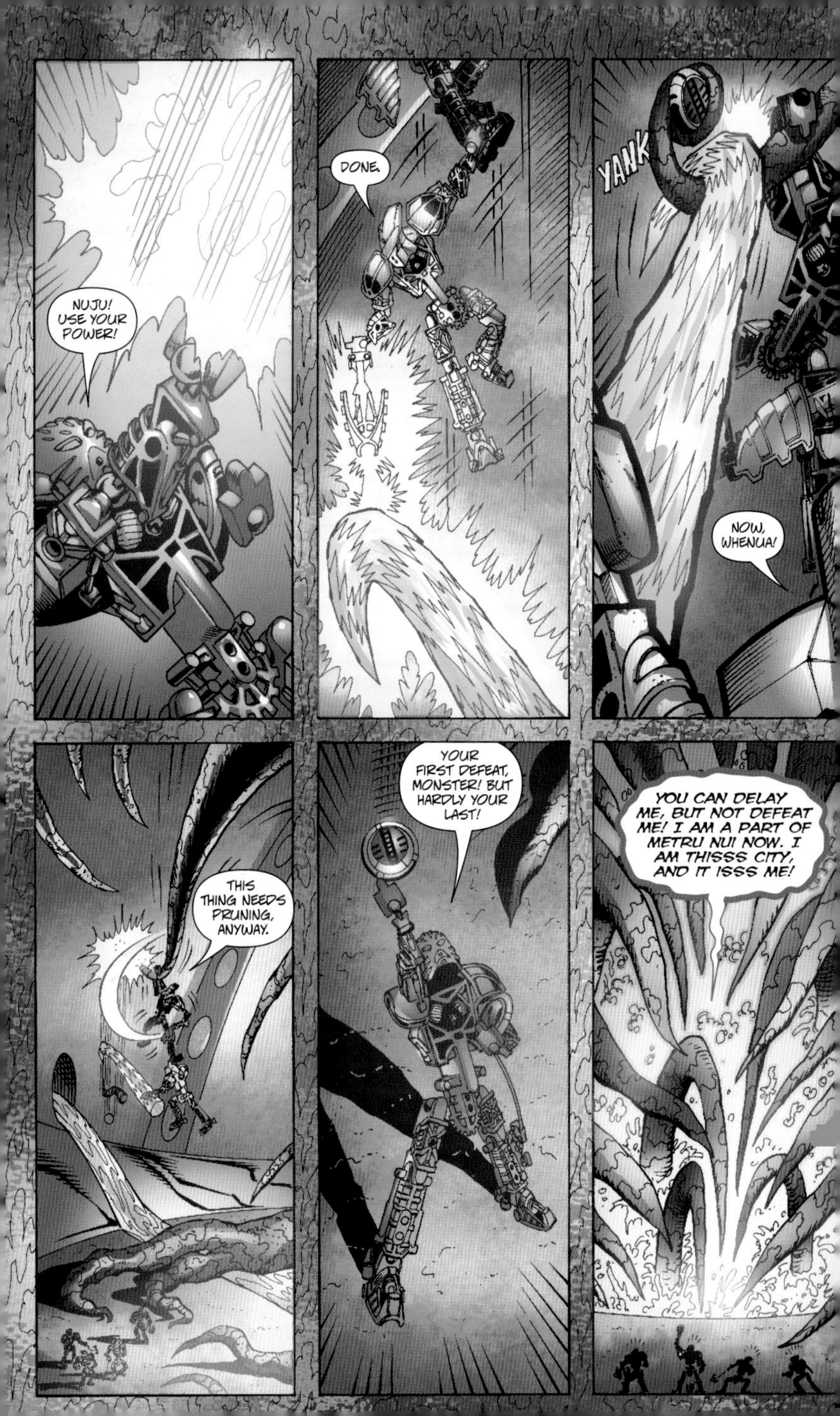
NUJU! USE YOUR POWER!
DONE.
YANK
NOW, WHENUA!
THIS THING NEEDS PRUNING, ANYWAY.
YOUR FIRST DEFEAT, MONSTER! BUT HARDLY YOUR LAST!
YOU CAN DELAY ME, BUT NOT DEFEAT ME! I AM A PART OF METRU NUI NOW. I AM THISSS CITY, AND IT ISSS ME!

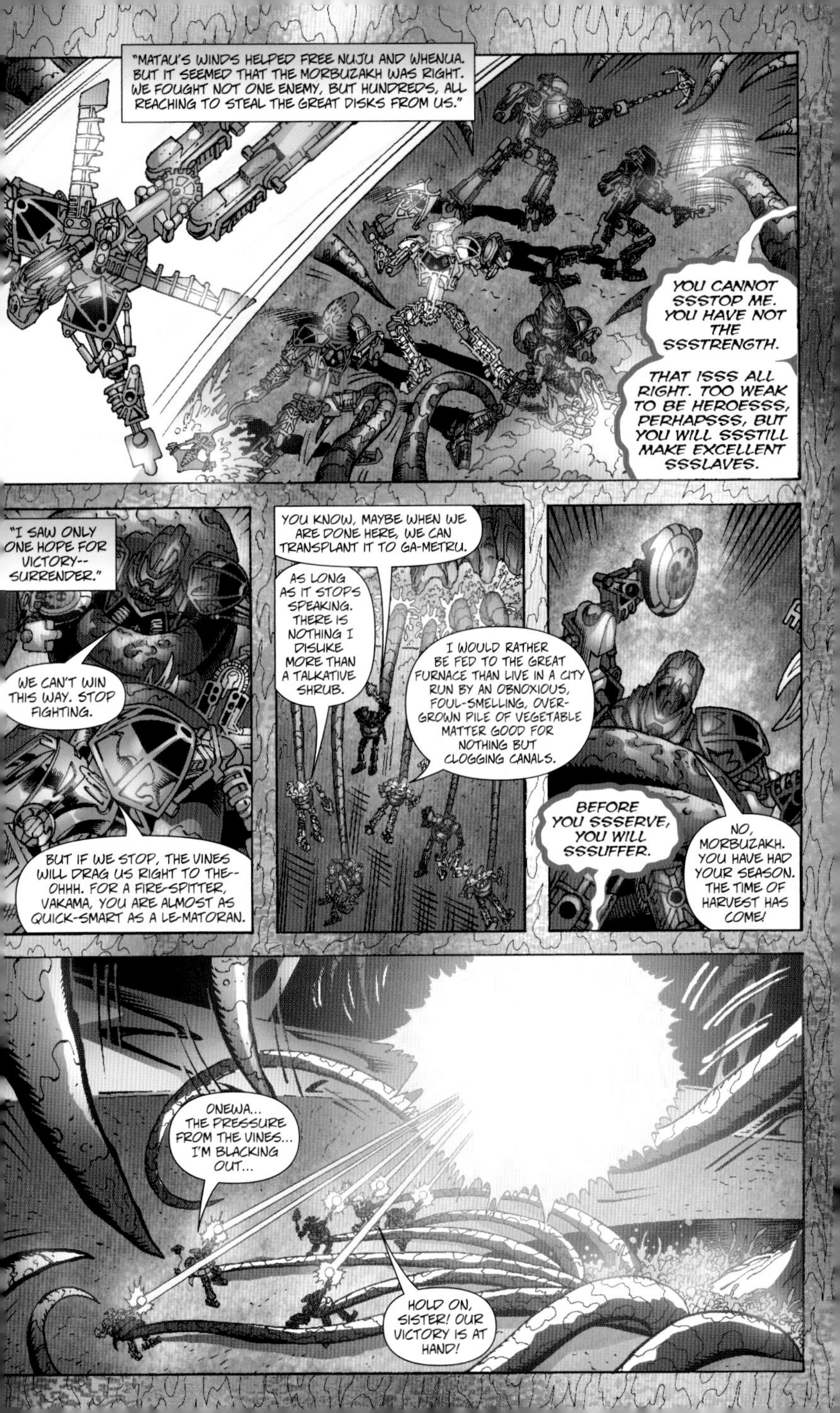
"MATAU'S WINDS HELPED FREE NUJU AND WHENUA. BUT IT SEEMED THAT THE MORBUZAKH WAS RIGHT. WE FOUGHT NOT ONE ENEMY, BUT HUNDREDS, ALL REACHING TO STEAL THE GREAT DISKS FROM US."
YOU CANNOT SSSTOP ME. YOU HAVE NOT THE SSSTRENGTH.
THAT ISSS ALL RIGHT. TOO WEAK TO BE HEROESSS, PERHAPSSS, BUT YOU WILL SSSTILL MAKE EXCELLENT SSSLAVES.
"I SAW ONLY ONE HOPE FOR VICTORY-- SURRENDER."
WE CAN'T WIN THIS WAY. STOP FIGHTING.
BUT IF WE STOP, THE VINES WILL DRAG US RIGHT TO THE-- OHHH. FOR A FIRE-SPITTER, VAKAMA, YOU ARE ALMOST AS QUICK-SMART AS A LE-MATORAN.
YOU KNOW, MAYBE WHEN WE ARE DONE HERE, WE CAN TRANSPLANT IT TO GA-METRU.
AS LONG AS IT STOPS SPEAKING. THERE IS NOTHING I DISLIKE MORE THAN A TALKATIVE SHRUB.
I WOULD RATHER BE FED TO THE GREAT FURNACE THAN LIVE IN A CITY RUN BY AN OBNOXIOUS, FOUL-SMELLING, OVER-GROWN PILE OF VEGETABLE MATTER GOOD FOR NOTHING BUT CLOGGING CANALS.
BEFORE YOU SSSERVE, YOU WILL SSSUFFER.
NO, MORBUZAKH. YOU HAVE HAD YOUR SEASON. THE TIME OF HARVEST HAS COME!
ONEWA... THE PRESSURE FROM THE VINES... I'M BLACKING OUT...
HOLD ON, SISTER! OUR VICTORY IS AT HAND!

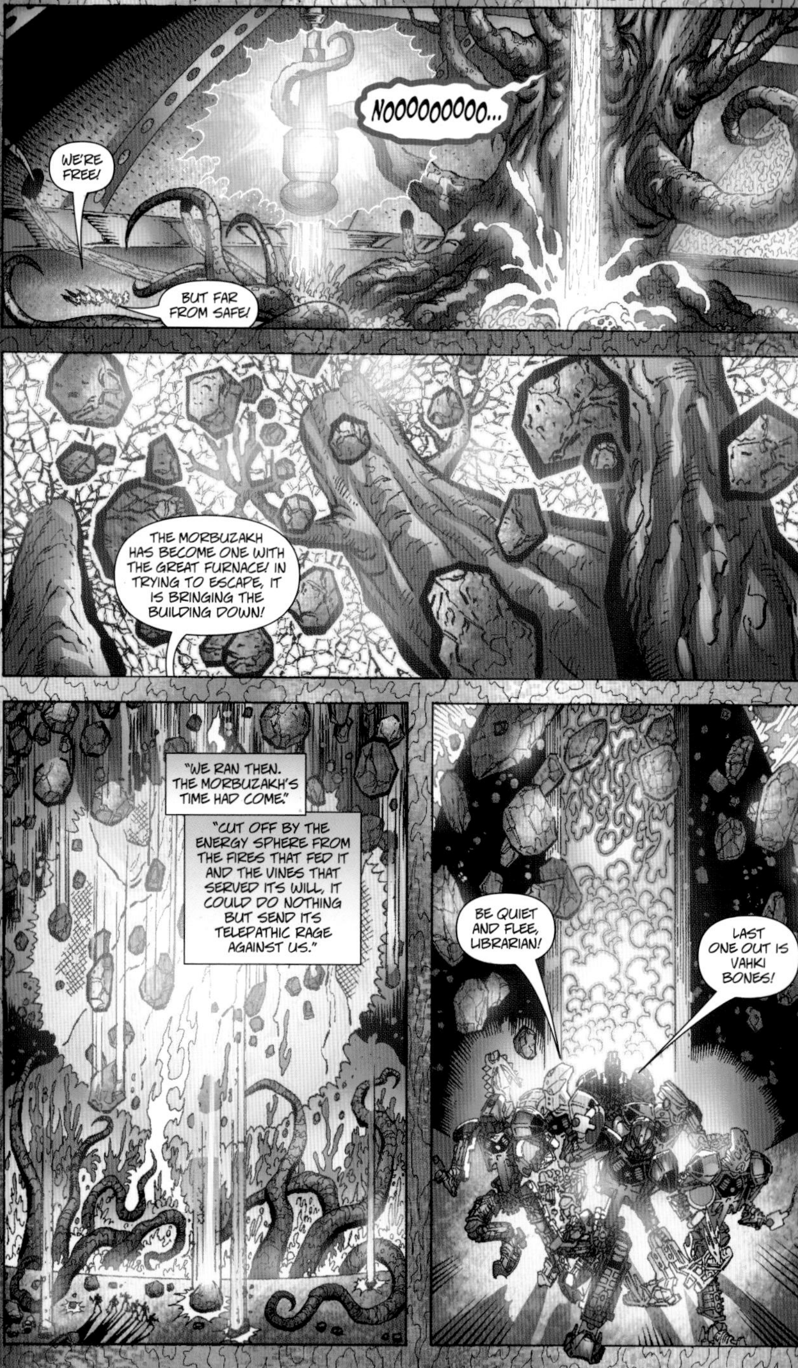
NOOOOOOOO...
WE'RE FREE!
BUT FAR FROM SAFE!
THE MORBUZAKH HAS BECOME ONE WITH THE GREAT FURNACE! IN TRYING TO ESCAPE, IT IS BRINGING THE BUILDING DOWN!
"WE RAN THEN. THE MORBUZAKH'S TIME HAD COME."
"CUT OFF BY THE ENERGY SPHERE FROM THE FIRES THAT FED IT AND THE VINES THAT SERVED ITS WILL, IT COULD DO NOTHING BUT SEND ITS TELEPATHIC RAGE AGAINST US."
BE QUIET AND FLEE, LIBRARIAN!
LAST ONE OUT IS VAHKI BONES!

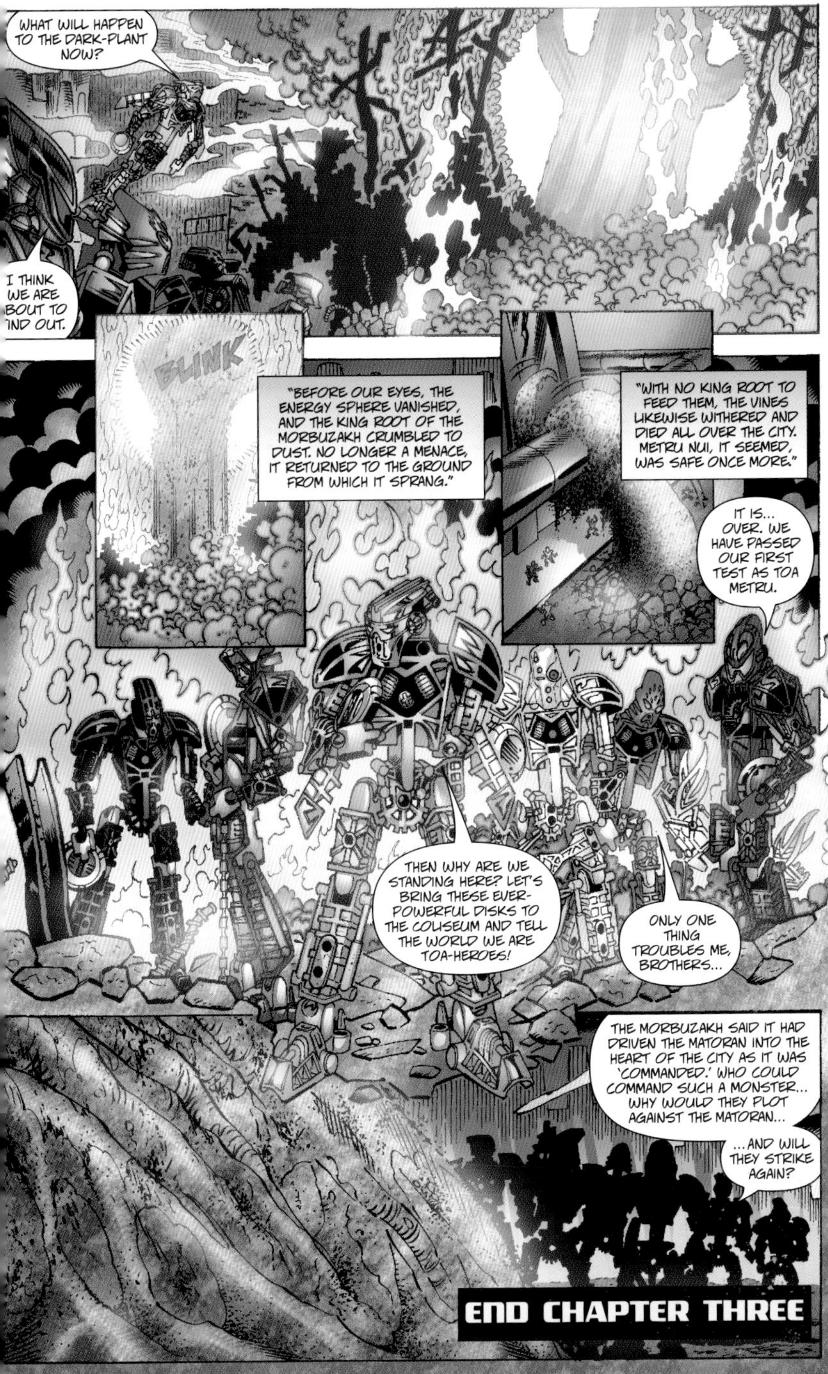
WHAT WILL HAPPEN TO THE DARK-PLANT NOW?
I THINK WE ARE BOUT TO IND OUT.
BLINK
"BEFORE OUR EYES, THE ENERGY SPHERE VANISHED, AND THE KING ROOT OF THE MORBUZAKH CRUMBLED TO DUST. NO LONGER A MENACE, IT RETURNED TO THE GROUND FROM WHICH IT SPRANG."
"WITH NO KING ROOT TO FEED THEM, THE VINES LIKEWISE WITHERED AND DIED ALL OVER THE CITY. METRU NUI, IT SEEMED, WAS SAFE ONCE MORE."
IT IS... OVER. WE HAVE PASSED OUR FIRST TEST AS TOA METRU.
THEN WHY ARE WE STANDING HERE? LET'S BRING THESE EVER-POWERFUL DISKS TO THE COLISEUM AND TELL THE WORLD WE ARE TOA-HEROES!
ONLY ONE THING TROUBLES ME, BROTHERS...
THE MORBUZAKH SAID IT HAD DRIVEN THE MATORAN INTO THE HEART OF THE CITY AS IT WAS 'COMMANDED.' WHO COULD COMMAND SUCH A MONSTER... WHY WOULD THEY PLOT AGAINST THE MATORAN...
...AND WILL THEY STRIKE AGAIN?
END CHAPTER THREE

CITY OF LEGENDS
CHAPTER FOUR

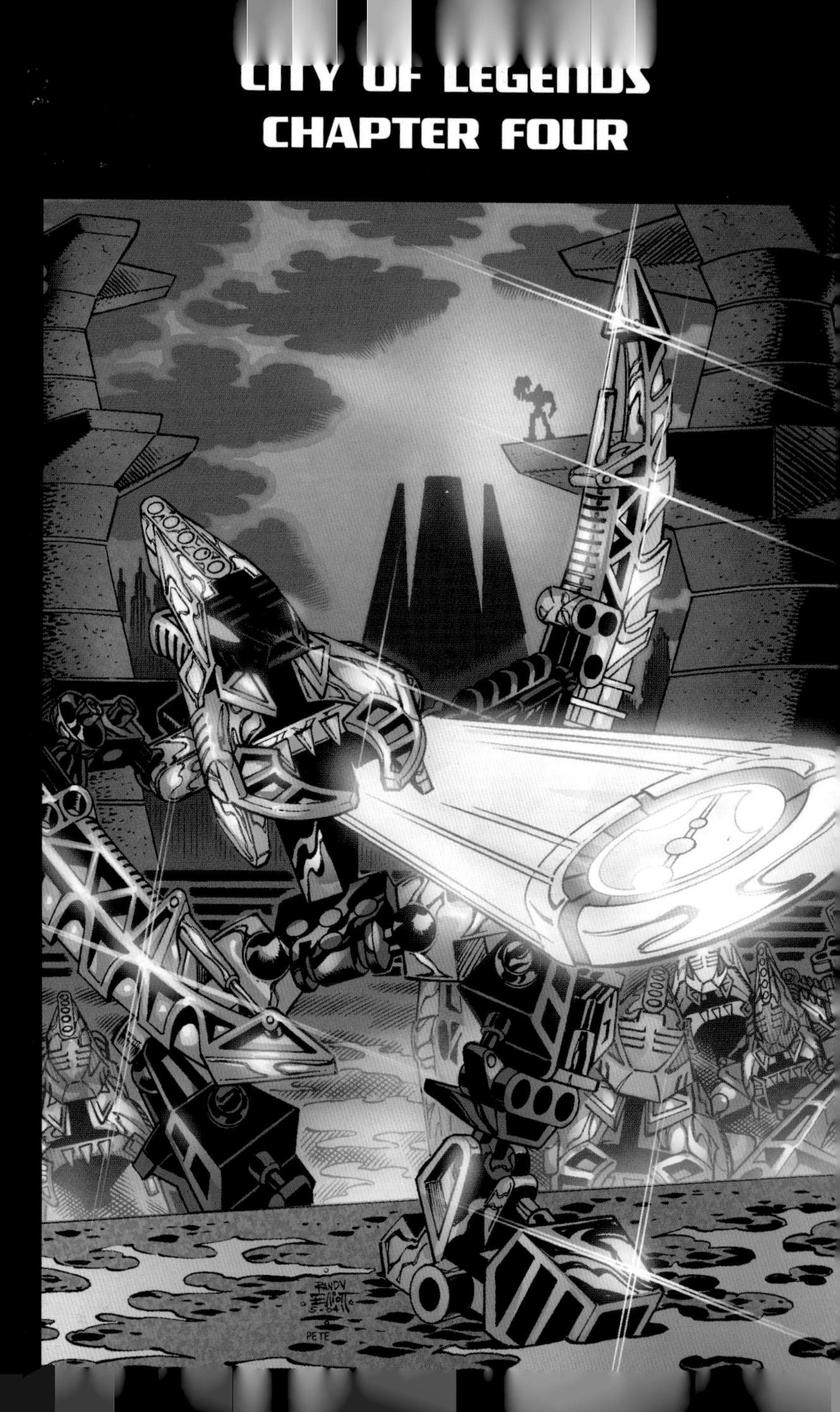

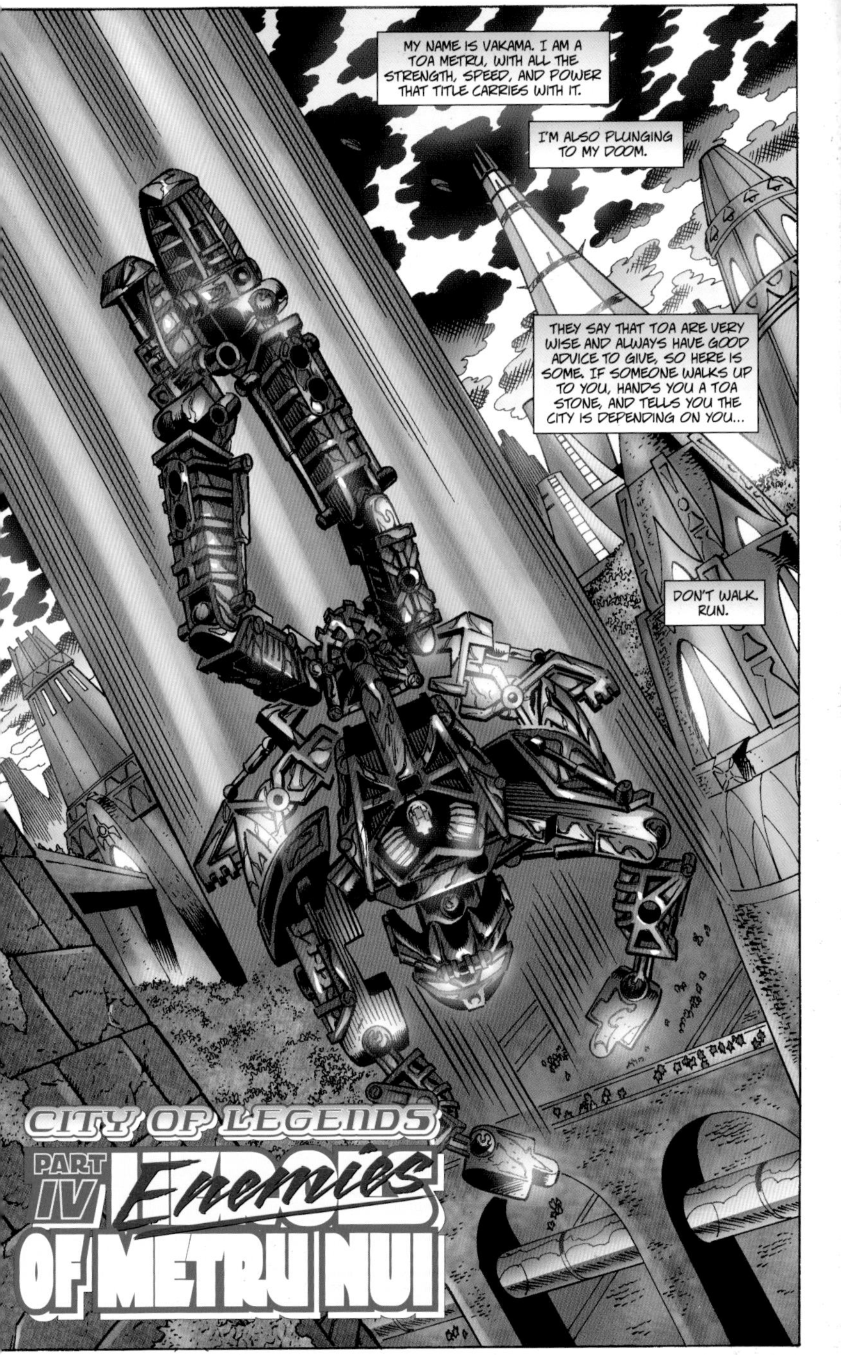
MY NAME IS VAKAMA. I AM A TOA METRU, WITH ALL THE STRENGTH, SPEED, AND POWER THAT TITLE CARRIES WITH IT.
I'M ALSO PLUNGING TO MY DOOM.
THEY SAY THAT TOA ARE VERY WISE AND ALWAYS HAVE GOOD ADVICE TO GIVE, SO HERE IS SOME. IF SOMEONE WALKS UP TO YOU, HANDS YOU A TOA STONE, AND TELLS YOU THE CITY IS DEPENDING ON YOU...
DON'T WALK. RUN.
CITY OF LEGENDS
PART IV
HEROES
Enemies
OF METRU NUI

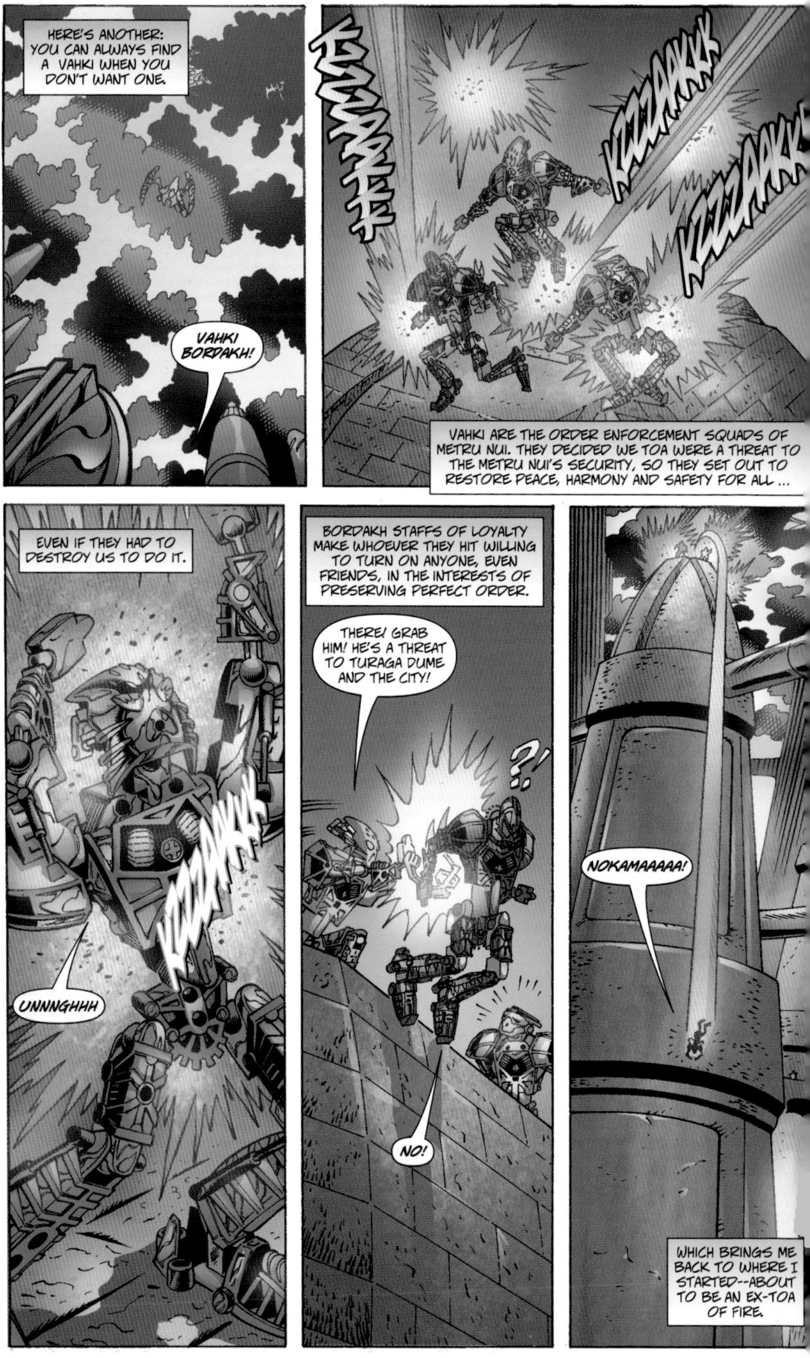
HERE'S ANOTHER: YOU CAN ALWAYS FIND A VAHKI WHEN YOU DON'T WANT ONE.
VAHKI BORDAKH!
KZZZAKKK
KZZZAKKK
VAHKI ARE THE ORDER ENFORCEMENT SQUADS OF METRU NUI. THEY DECIDED WE TOA WERE A THREAT TO THE METRU NUI'S SECURITY, SO THEY SET OUT TO RESTORE PEACE, HARMONY AND SAFETY FOR ALL ...
EVEN IF THEY HAD TO DESTROY US TO DO IT.
KZZZAKKK
UNNNGHHH
BORDAKH STAFFS OF LOYALTY MAKE WHOEVER THEY HIT WILLING TO TURN ON ANYONE, EVEN FRIENDS, IN THE INTERESTS OF PRESERVING PERFECT ORDER.
THERE! GRAB HIM! HE'S A THREAT TO TURAGA DUME AND THE CITY!
?!
NO!
NOKAMAAAAA!
WHICH BRINGS ME BACK TO WHERE I STARTED--ABOUT TO BE AN EX-TOA OF FIRE.

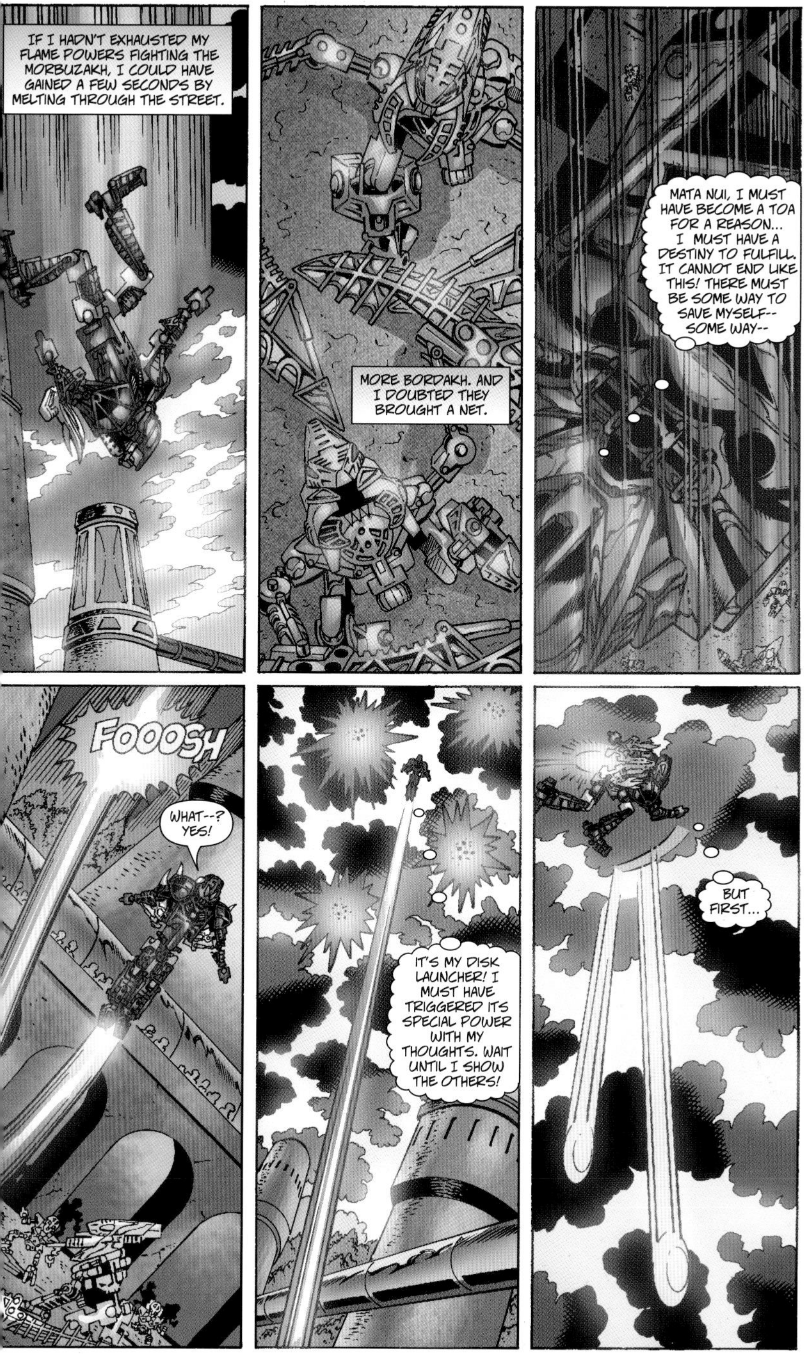
IF I HADN'T EXHAUSTED MY FLAME POWERS FIGHTING THE MORBUZAKH, I COULD HAVE GAINED A FEW SECONDS BY MELTING THROUGH THE STREET.
MORE BORDAKH. AND I DOUBTED THEY BROUGHT A NET.
MATA NUI, I MUST HAVE BECOME A TOA FOR A REASON... I MUST HAVE A DESTINY TO FULFILL. IT CANNOT END LIKE THIS! THERE MUST BE SOME WAY TO SAVE MYSELF-- SOME WAY--
FOOOSH
WHAT--? YES!
IT'S MY DISK LAUNCHER! I MUST HAVE TRIGGERED ITS SPECIAL POWER WITH MY THOUGHTS. WAIT UNTIL I SHOW THE OTHERS!
BUT FIRST...

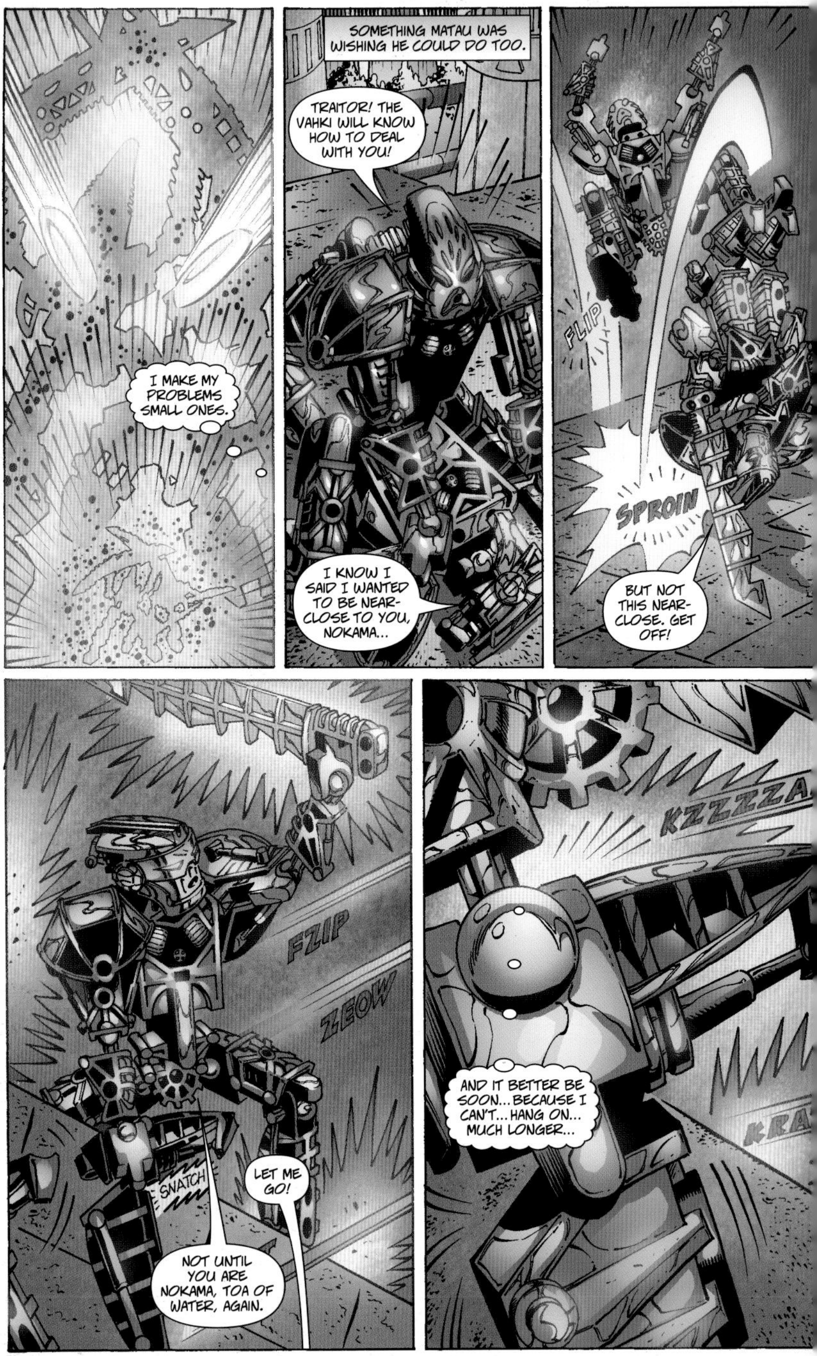
I MAKE MY PROBLEMS SMALL ONES.
SOMETHING MATAU WAS WISHING HE COULD DO TOO.
TRAITOR! THE VAHKI WILL KNOW HOW TO DEAL WITH YOU!
I KNOW I SAID I WANTED TO BE NEAR-CLOSE TO YOU, NOKAMA...
FLIP
SPROIN
BUT NOT THIS NEAR-CLOSE. GET OFF!
FZIP
ZEOW
SNATCH
LET ME GO!
NOT UNTIL YOU ARE NOKAMA, TOA OF WATER, AGAIN.
KZZZZA
AND IT BETTER BE SOON... BECAUSE I CAN'T... HANG ON... MUCH LONGER...

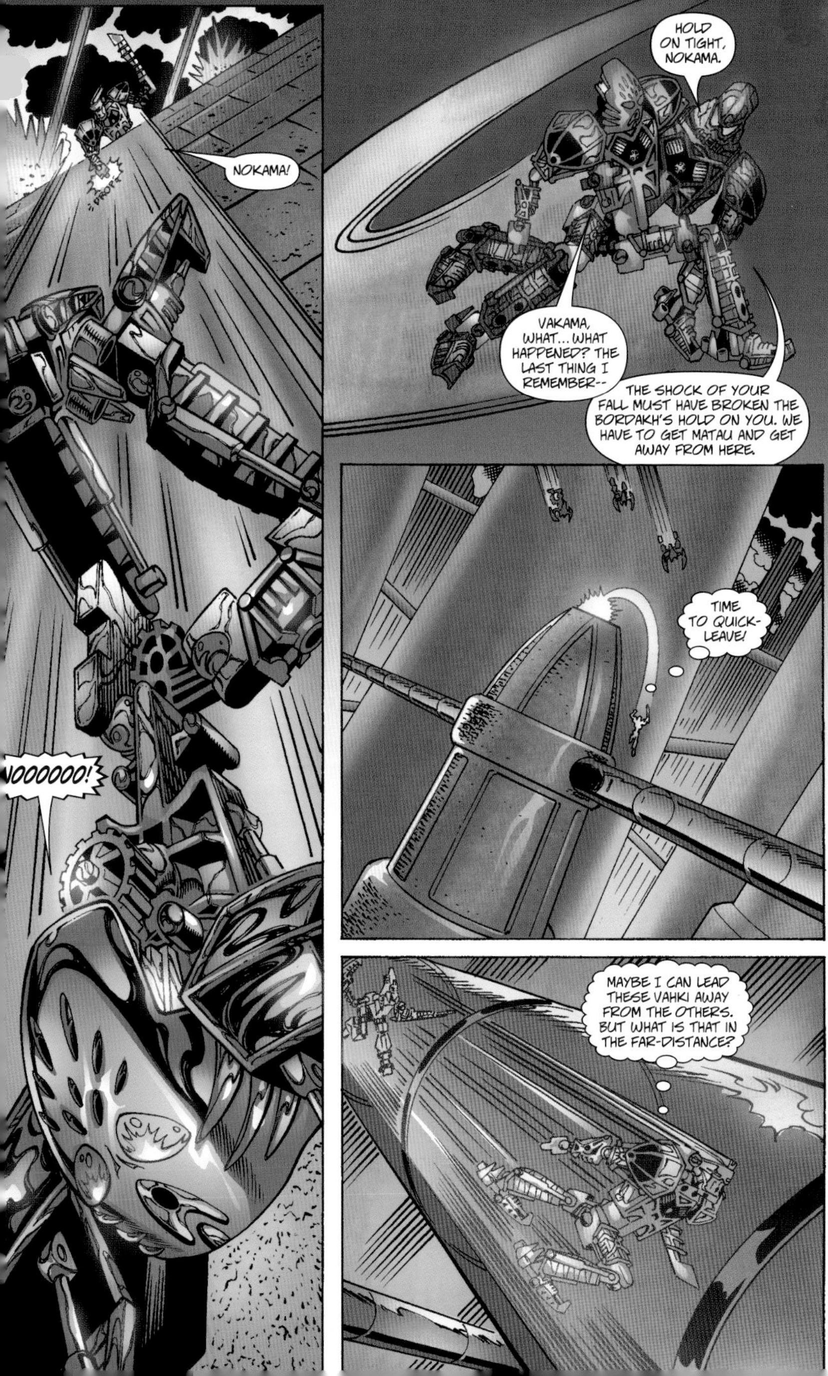
NOKAMA!
DROP
NOOOOOO!
HOLD ON TIGHT, NOKAMA.
VAKAMA, WHAT... WHAT HAPPENED? THE LAST THING I REMEMBER--
THE SHOCK OF YOUR FALL MUST HAVE BROKEN THE BORDAKH'S HOLD ON YOU. WE HAVE TO GET MATAU AND GET AWAY FROM HERE.
TIME TO QUICK-LEAVE!
MAYBE I CAN LEAD THESE VAHKI AWAY FROM THE OTHERS. BUT WHAT IS THAT IN THE FAR-DISTANCE?

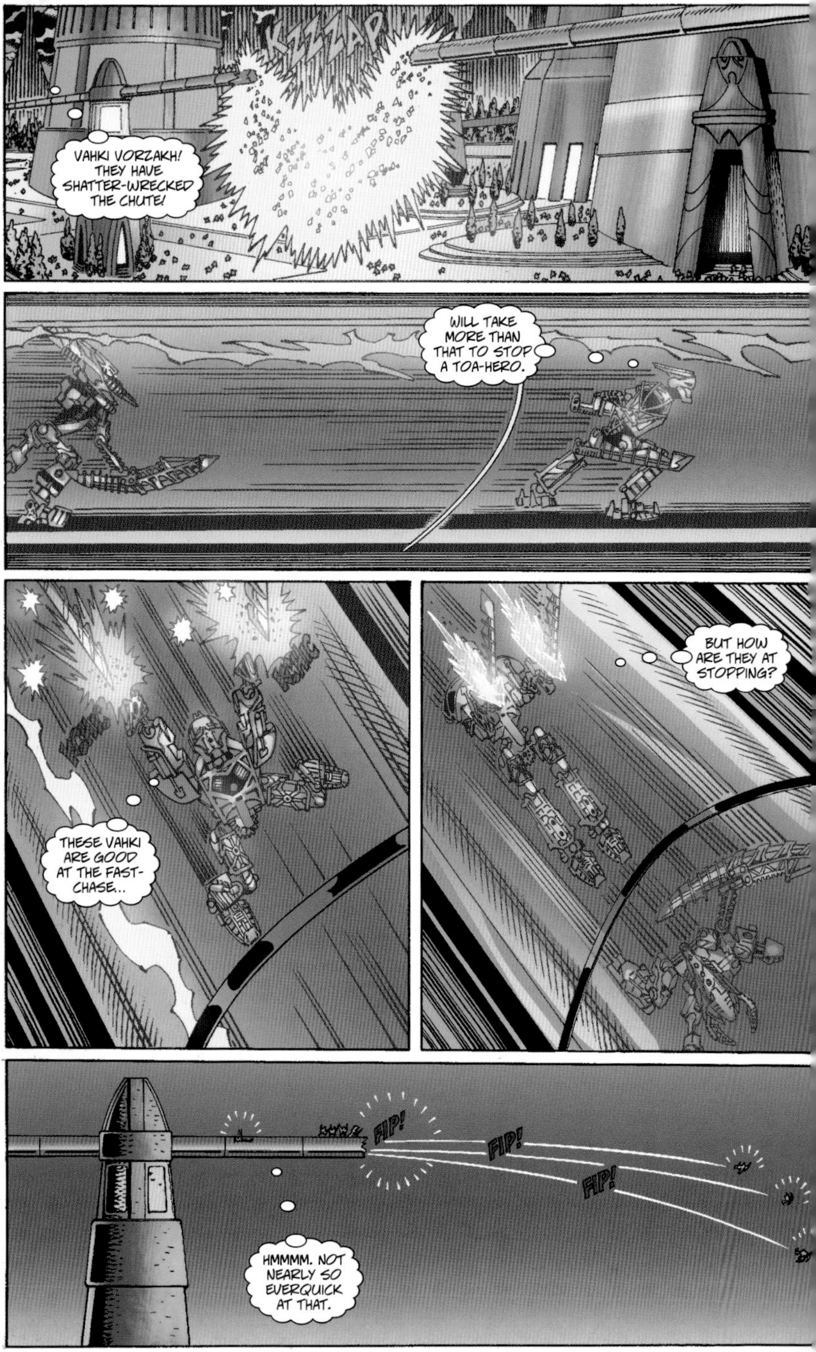
KZZZAP
VAHKI VORZAKH! THEY HAVE SHATTER-WRECKED THE CHUTE!
WILL TAKE MORE THAN THAT TO STOP A TOA-HERO.
THESE VAHKI ARE GOOD AT THE FAST-CHASE...
BUT HOW ARE THEY AT STOPPING?
FIP!
FIP!
FIP!
HMMMM. NOT NEARLY SO EVERQUICK AT THAT.

WHILE THIS WAS GOING ON, ONEWA, NUJU, AND WHENUA WERE BEING MARCHED THROUGH UNDERGROUND TUNNELS TO AN UNKNOWN DESTINATION.

WHEN I GIVE THE WORD, WE MAKE A BREAK FOR THE SURFACE.

BAD IDEA, ONEWA. IN ALL OF THEIR HISTORY, THE RORZAKH HAVE NEVER FAILED TO CAPTURE A RUNNER.

I DON'T SEE YOU COMING UP WITH ANY BETTER IDEAS, LIBRARIAN!

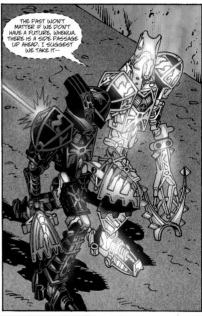

THE PAST WON'T MATTER IF WE DON'T HAVE A FUTURE, WHENUA. THERE IS A SIDE PASSAGE UP AHEAD. I SUGGEST WE TAKE IT--

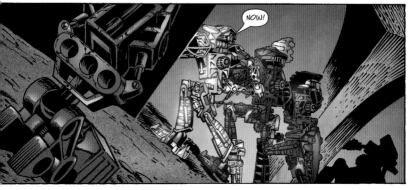

NOW!

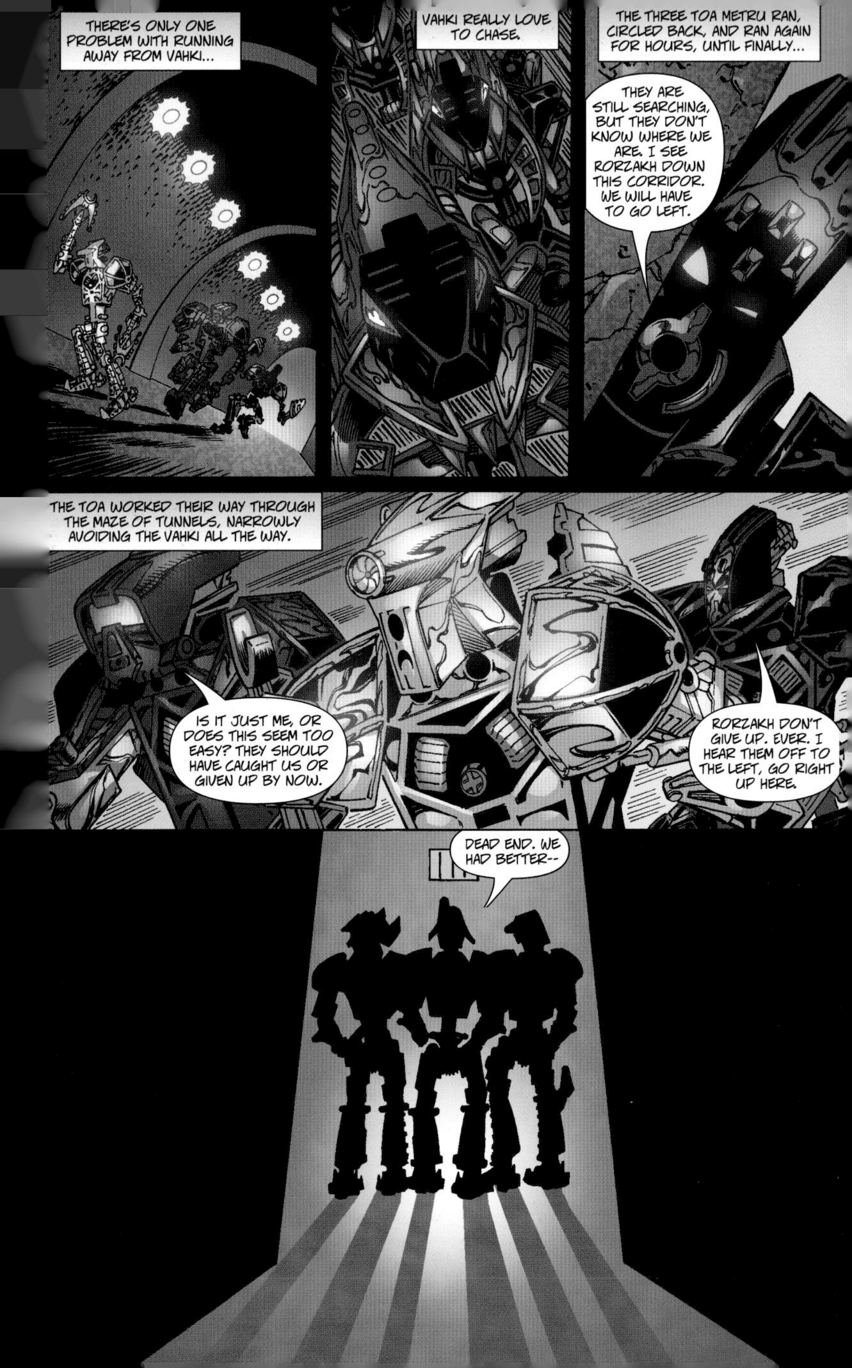
THERE'S ONLY ONE PROBLEM WITH RUNNING AWAY FROM VAHKI...
VAHKI REALLY LOVE TO CHASE.
THE THREE TOA METRU RAN, CIRCLED BACK, AND RAN AGAIN FOR HOURS, UNTIL FINALLY...
THEY ARE STILL SEARCHING, BUT THEY DON'T KNOW WHERE WE ARE. I SEE RORZAKH DOWN THIS CORRIDOR. WE WILL HAVE TO GO LEFT.
THE TOA WORKED THEIR WAY THROUGH THE MAZE OF TUNNELS, NARROWLY AVOIDING THE VAHKI ALL THE WAY.
IS IT JUST ME, OR DOES THIS SEEM TOO EASY? THEY SHOULD HAVE CAUGHT US OR GIVEN UP BY NOW.
RORZAKH DON'T GIVE UP. EVER. I HEAR THEM OFF TO THE LEFT, GO RIGHT UP HERE.
DEAD END. WE HAD BETTER--

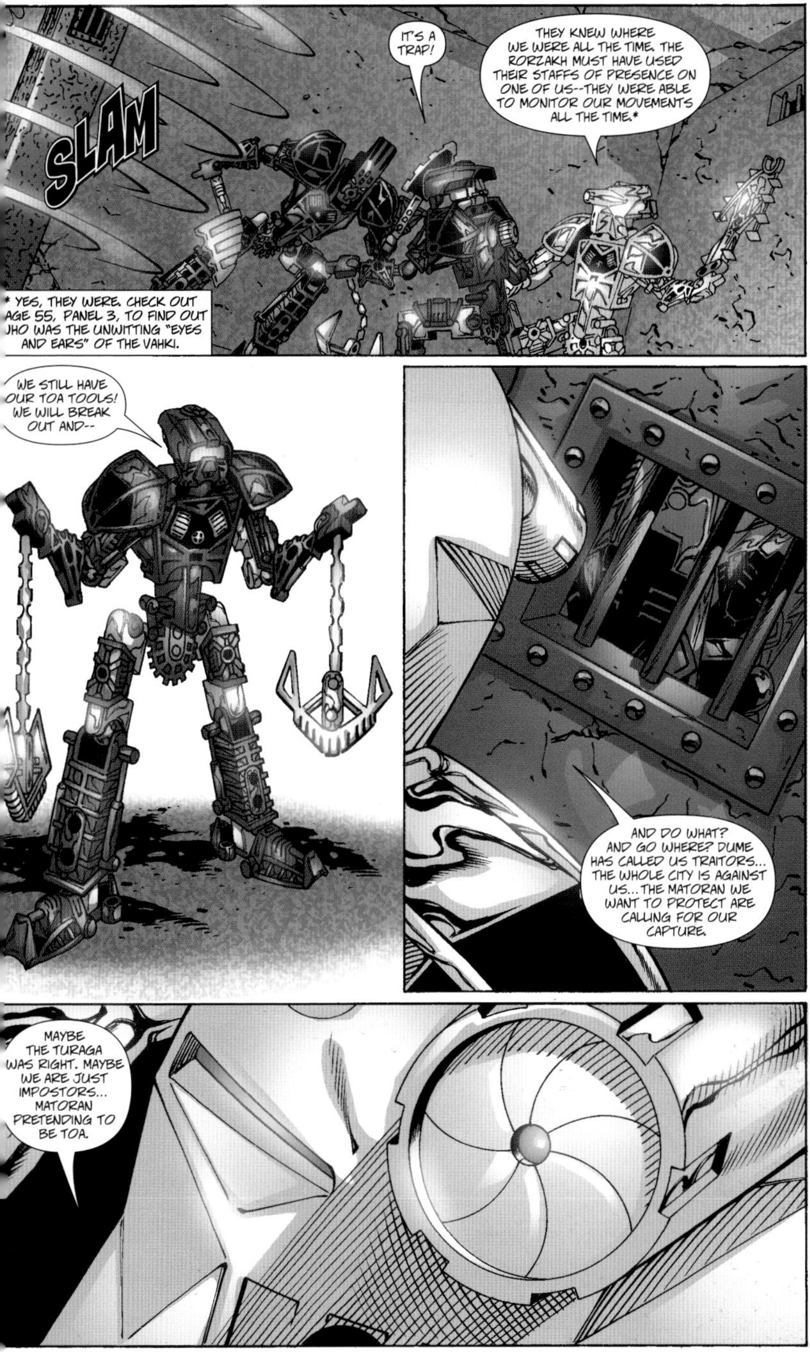
SLAM
IT'S A TRAP!
THEY KNEW WHERE WE WERE ALL THE TIME. THE RORZAKH MUST HAVE USED THEIR STAFFS OF PRESENCE ON ONE OF US--THEY WERE ABLE TO MONITOR OUR MOVEMENTS ALL THE TIME.*
* YES, THEY WERE. CHECK OUT AGE 55, PANEL 3, TO FIND OUT JHO WAS THE UNWITTING "EYES AND EARS" OF THE VAHKI.
WE STILL HAVE OUR TOA TOOLS! WE WILL BREAK OUT AND--
AND DO WHAT? AND GO WHERE? DUME HAS CALLED US TRAITORS... THE WHOLE CITY IS AGAINST US... THE MATORAN WE WANT TO PROTECT ARE CALLING FOR OUR CAPTURE.
MAYBE THE TURAGA WAS RIGHT. MAYBE WE ARE JUST IMPOSTORS... MATORAN PRETENDING TO BE TOA.

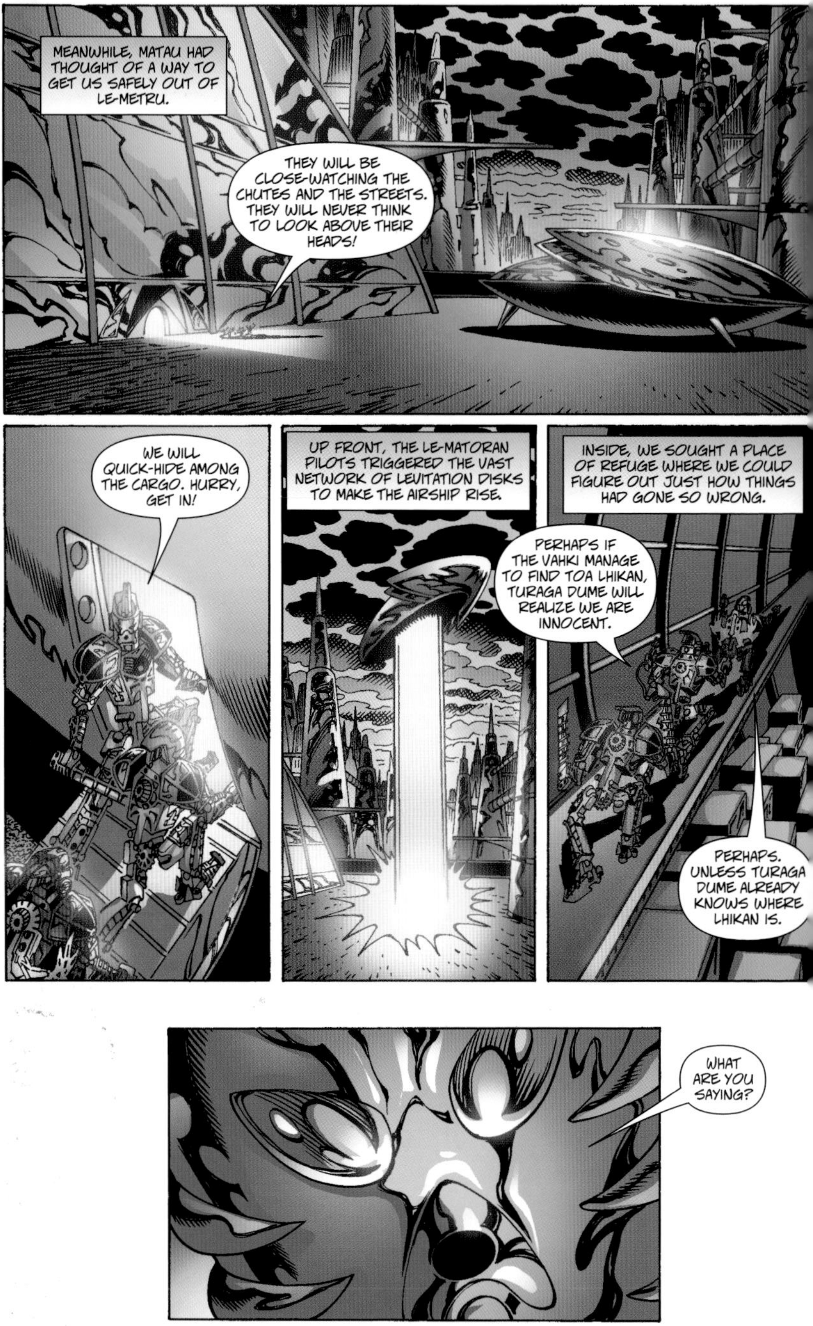
MEANWHILE, MATAU HAD THOUGHT OF A WAY TO GET US SAFELY OUT OF LE-METRU.
THEY WILL BE CLOSE-WATCHING THE CHUTES AND THE STREETS. THEY WILL NEVER THINK TO LOOK ABOVE THEIR HEADS!
WE WILL QUICK-HIDE AMONG THE CARGO. HURRY, GET IN!
UP FRONT, THE LE-MATORAN PILOTS TRIGGERED THE VAST NETWORK OF LEVITATION DISKS TO MAKE THE AIRSHIP RISE.
INSIDE, WE SOUGHT A PLACE OF REFUGE WHERE WE COULD FIGURE OUT JUST HOW THINGS HAD GONE SO WRONG.
PERHAPS IF THE VAHKI MANAGE TO FIND TOA LHIKAN, TURAGA DUME WILL REALIZE WE ARE INNOCENT.
PERHAPS. UNLESS TURAGA DUME ALREADY KNOWS WHERE LHIKAN IS.
WHAT ARE YOU SAYING?

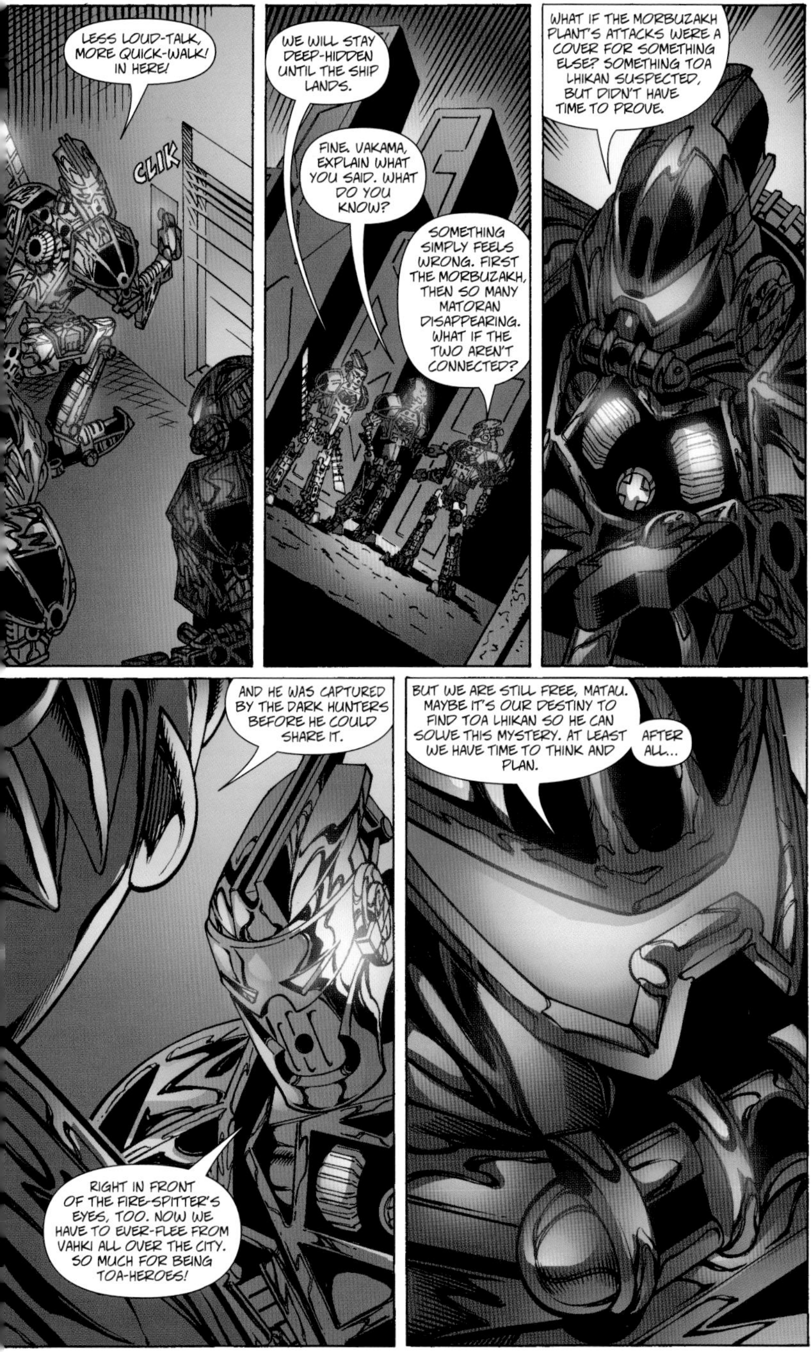
LESS LOUD-TALK, MORE QUICK-WALK! IN HERE!
CLIK
WE WILL STAY DEEP-HIDDEN UNTIL THE SHIP LANDS.
FINE. VAKAMA, EXPLAIN WHAT YOU SAID. WHAT DO YOU KNOW?
SOMETHING SIMPLY FEELS WRONG. FIRST THE MORBUZAKH, THEN SO MANY MATORAN DISAPPEARING. WHAT IF THE TWO AREN'T CONNECTED?
WHAT IF THE MORBUZAKH PLANT'S ATTACKS WERE A COVER FOR SOMETHING ELSE? SOMETHING TOA LHIKAN SUSPECTED, BUT DIDN'T HAVE TIME TO PROVE.
AND HE WAS CAPTURED BY THE DARK HUNTERS BEFORE HE COULD SHARE IT.
RIGHT IN FRONT OF THE FIRE-SPITTER'S EYES, TOO. NOW WE HAVE TO EVER-FLEE FROM VAHKI ALL OVER THE CITY. SO MUCH FOR BEING TOA-HEROES!
BUT WE ARE STILL FREE, MATAU. MAYBE IT'S OUR DESTINY TO FIND TOA LHIKAN SO HE CAN SOLVE THIS MYSTERY. AT LEAST WE HAVE TIME TO THINK AND PLAN.
AFTER ALL...

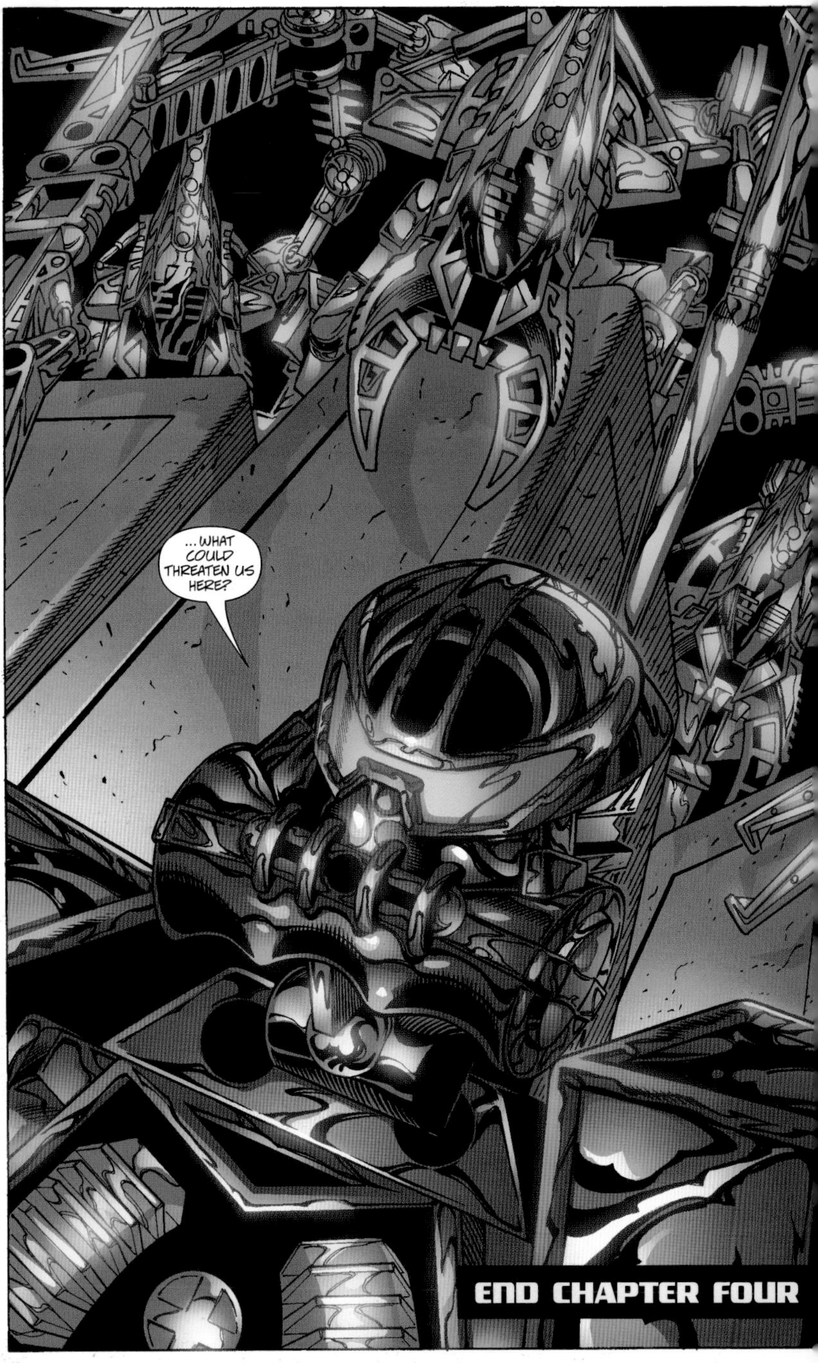
...WHAT COULD THREATEN US HERE?
END CHAPTER FOUR

CITY OF LEGENDS
CHAPTER FIVE

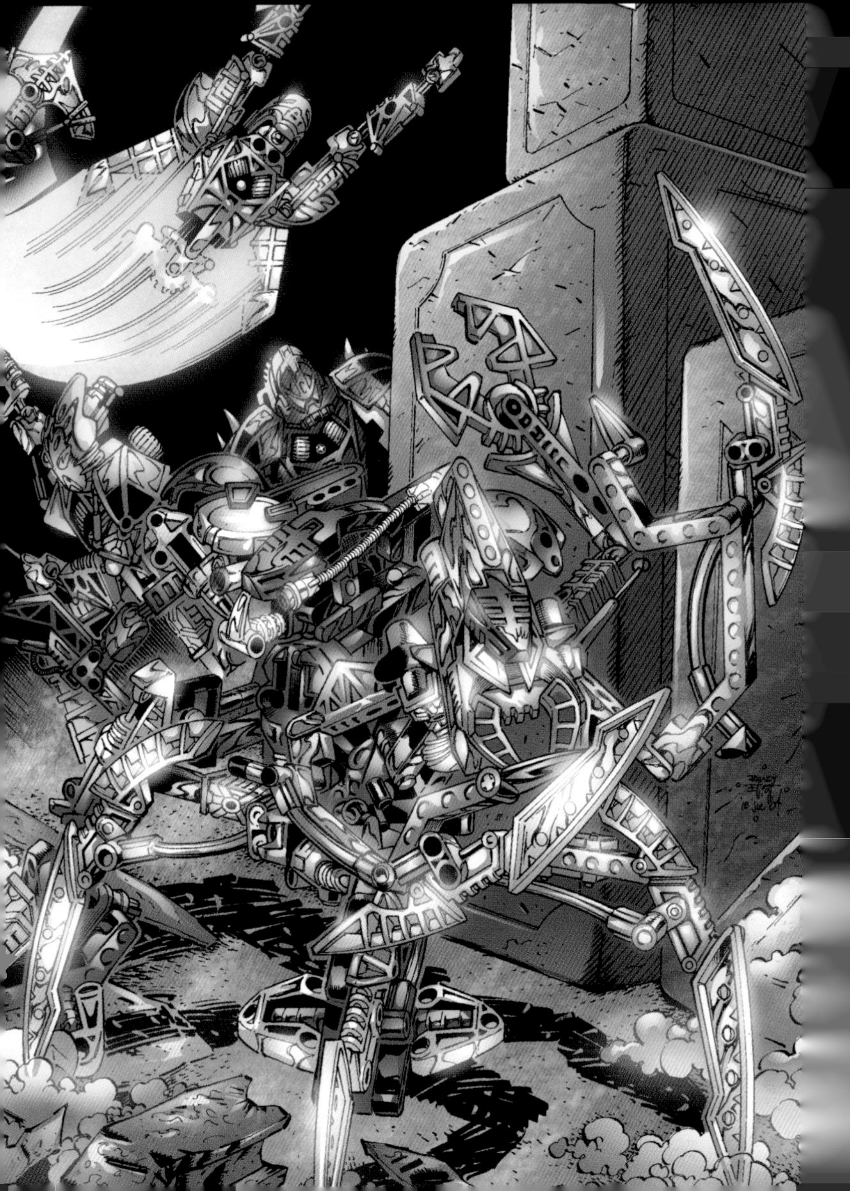

ULTIMATE POWER

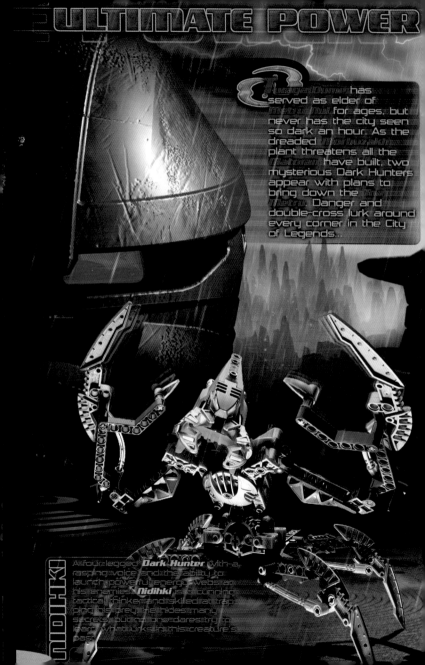

Turaga Dume has served as elder of *Metru Nui* for ages, but never has the city seen so dark an hour. As the dreaded *Morbuzakh* plant threatens all the *Matoran* have built, two mysterious Dark Hunters appear with plans to bring down the *Great Metru*. Danger and double-cross lurk around every corner in the City of Legends...

NIDHIKI

A four-legged **Dark Hunter** with a rasping voice and the ability to launch powerful energy webs at his enemies, *Nidhiki* is a cunning tactical thinker and skilled at trapping his prey. He hides many secrets, but no one dares try to learn what lurks in this creature's past.

... A CITY of LEGENDS!

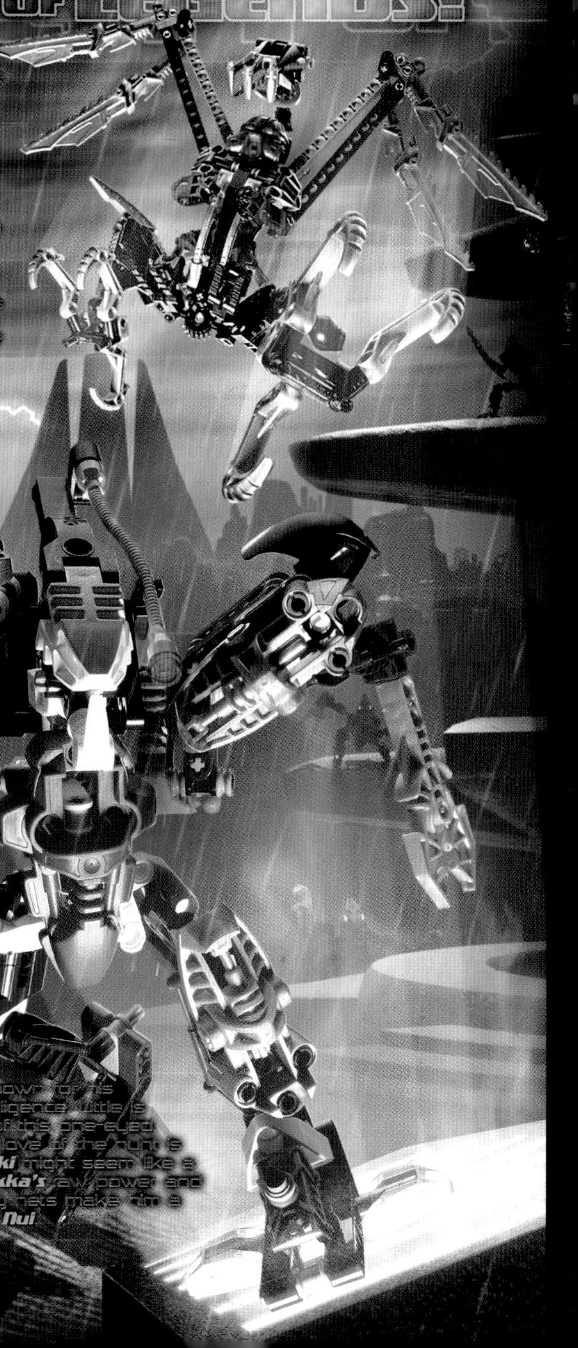

TURAGA DUME AND NIVAWK

Turaga Dume is the powerful elder of ***Metru Nui***. It's his job to protect the ***Matoran*** from danger and command the ***Vahki*** force. With his pet, the winged ***Nivawk***, ***Dume*** keeps watch from his chamber atop the Coliseum. But is he a friend to the ***Toa***... or an enemy?

KREKKA

This ***Dark Hunter*** is known for his strength, if not his intelligence. Little is known of the history of this one-eyed ape-like being, but his love of the hunt is obvious. He and ***Nidihki*** might seem like a strange team, but ***Krekka's*** raw power and ability to launch energy nets make him a danger to all in ***Metru Nui***.

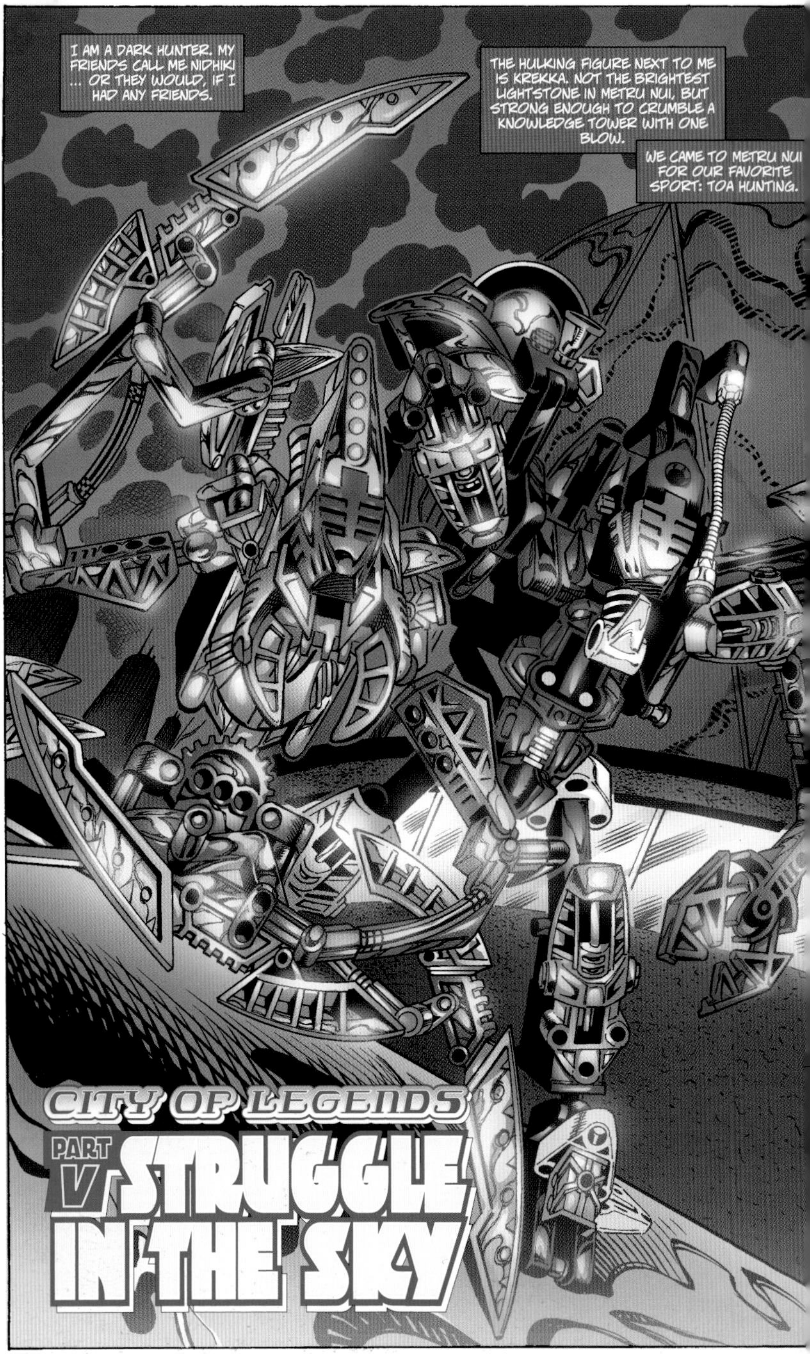
I AM A DARK HUNTER. MY FRIENDS CALL ME NIDHIKI ... OR THEY WOULD, IF I HAD ANY FRIENDS.
THE HULKING FIGURE NEXT TO ME IS KREKKA. NOT THE BRIGHTEST LIGHTSTONE IN METRU NUI, BUT STRONG ENOUGH TO CRUMBLE A KNOWLEDGE TOWER WITH ONE BLOW.
WE CAME TO METRU NUI FOR OUR FAVORITE SPORT: TOA HUNTING.
CITY OF LEGENDS
PART V STRUGGLE IN THE SKY

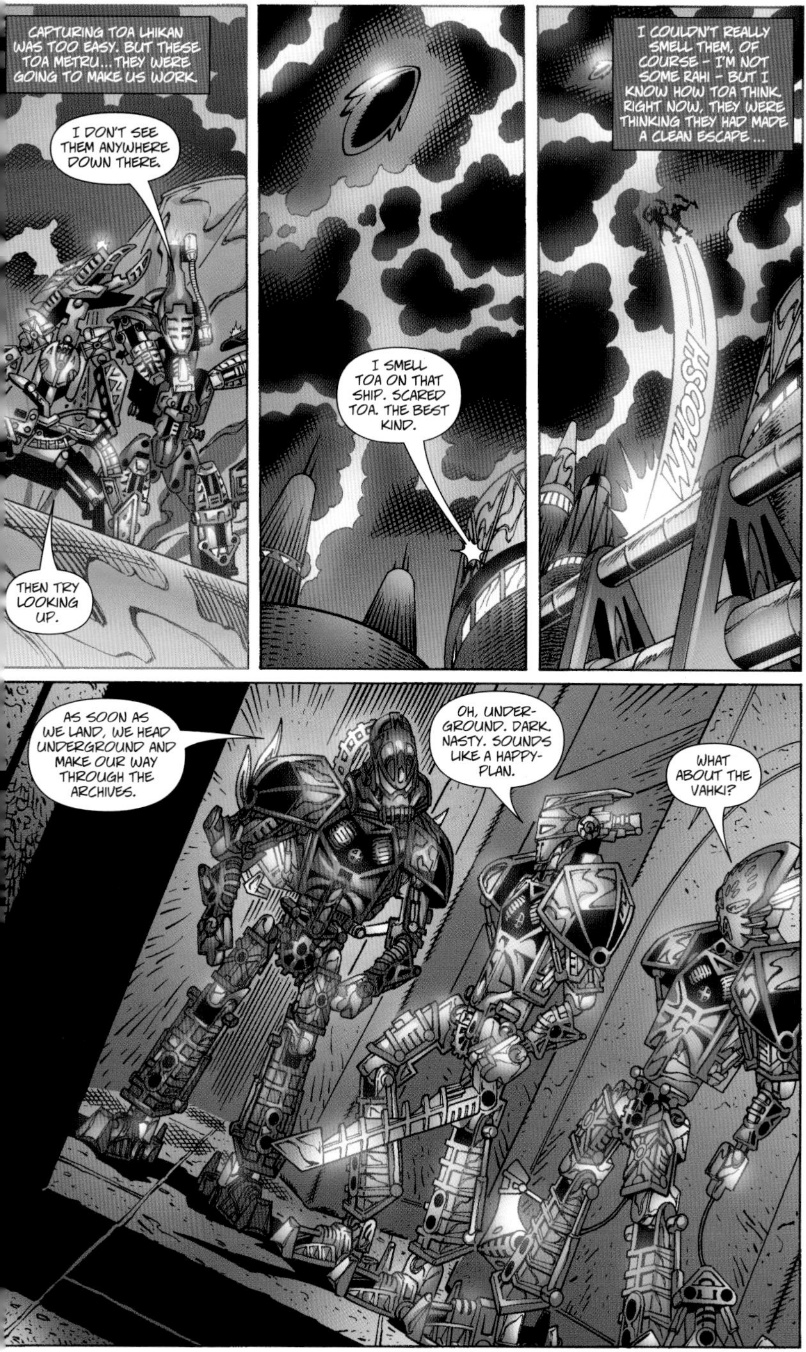
CAPTURING TOA LHIKAN WAS TOO EASY. BUT THESE TOA METRU... THEY WERE GOING TO MAKE US WORK.
I DON'T SEE THEM ANYWHERE DOWN THERE.
THEN TRY LOOKING UP.
I SMELL TOA ON THAT SHIP. SCARED TOA. THE BEST KIND.
I COULDN'T REALLY SMELL THEM, OF COURSE - I'M NOT SOME RAHI - BUT I KNOW HOW TOA THINK. RIGHT NOW, THEY WERE THINKING THEY HAD MADE A CLEAN ESCAPE...
WHOOSH
AS SOON AS WE LAND, WE HEAD UNDERGROUND AND MAKE OUR WAY THROUGH THE ARCHIVES.
OH, UNDER-GROUND. DARK. NASTY. SOUNDS LIKE A HAPPY-PLAN.
WHAT ABOUT THE VAHKI?

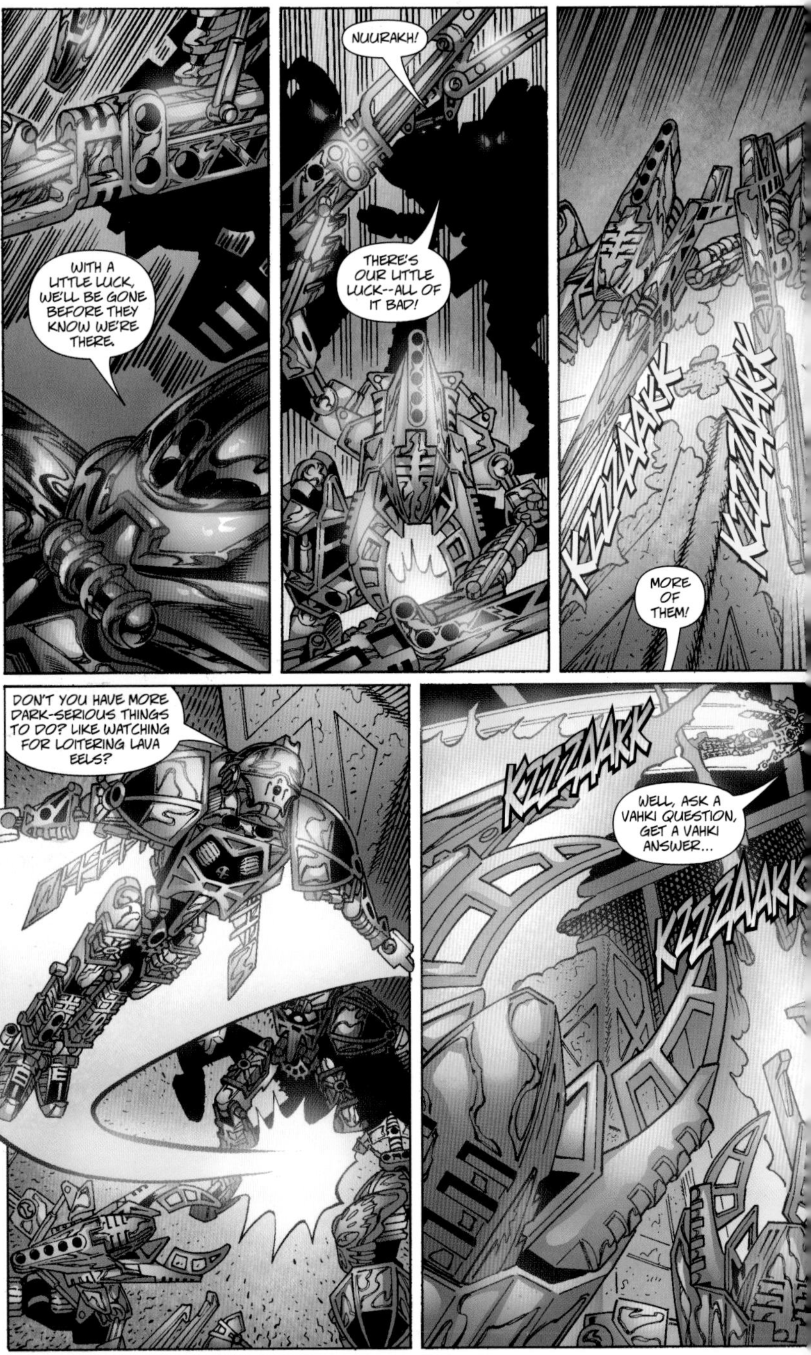

WITH A LITTLE LUCK, WE'LL BE GONE BEFORE THEY KNOW WE'RE THERE.
NUURAKH!
THERE'S OUR LITTLE LUCK--ALL OF IT BAD!
KZZZAAKK
KZZZAAKK
MORE OF THEM!
DON'T YOU HAVE MORE DARK-SERIOUS THINGS TO DO? LIKE WATCHING FOR LOITERING LAVA EELS?
KZZZAAKK
WELL, ASK A VAHKI QUESTION, GET A VAHKI ANSWER...
KZZZAAKK

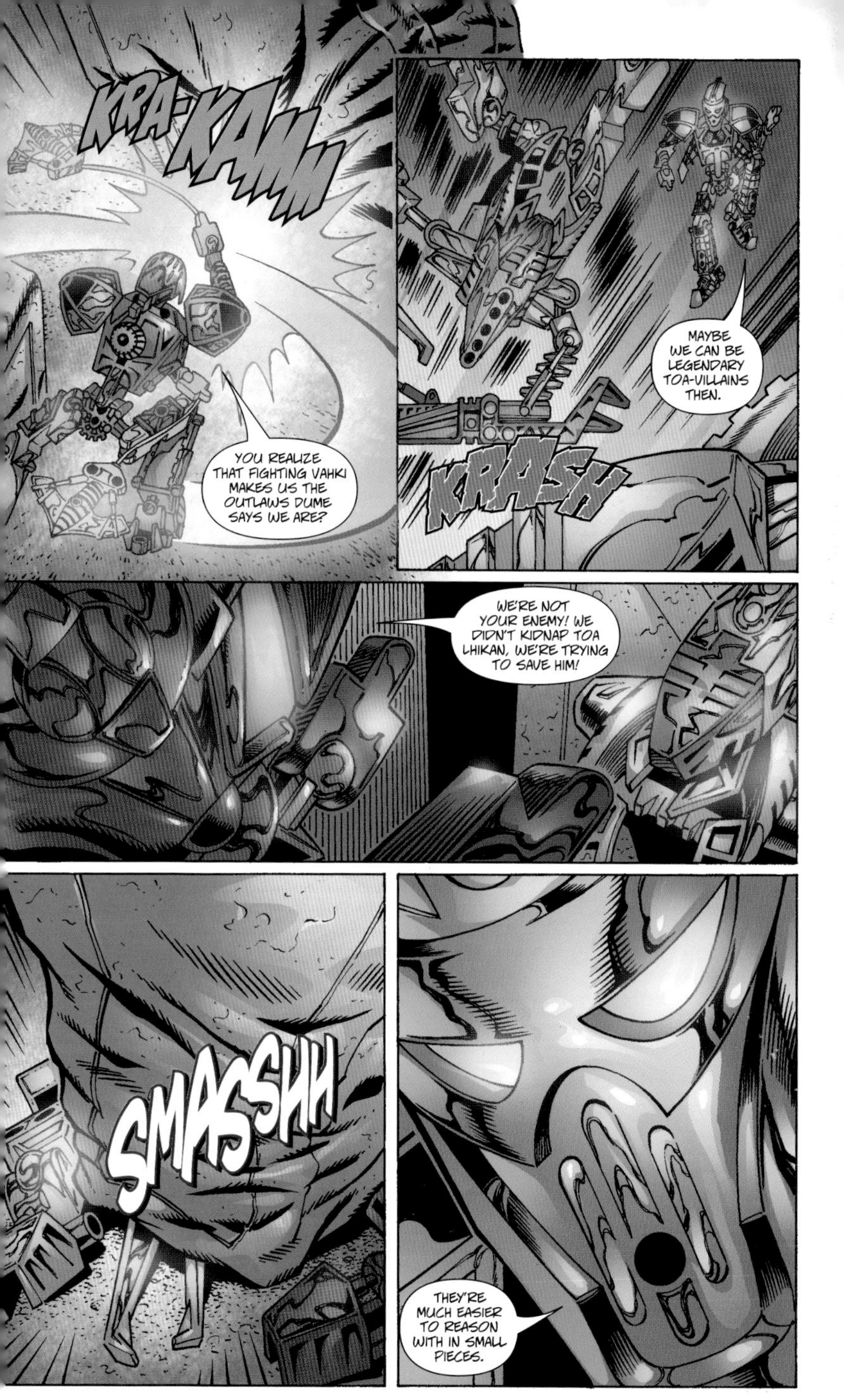
KRA-KAMM
YOU REALIZE THAT FIGHTING VAHKI MAKES US THE OUTLAWS DUME SAYS WE ARE?
MAYBE WE CAN BE LEGENDARY TOA-VILLAINS THEN.
KRASH
WE'RE NOT YOUR ENEMY! WE DIDN'T KIDNAP TOA LHIKAN, WE'RE TRYING TO SAVE HIM!
SMASHH
THEY'RE MUCH EASIER TO REASON WITH IN SMALL PIECES.

SORRY FOR THE INTERRUPTION, LITTLE TOA. BUT I NEVER COULD WAIT TO OPEN MY PRESENTS.

RRRIIIIPPPP

YOU! THE ONE WHO CAPTURED TOA LHIKAN!

YES, AND HE BEGGED FOR MERCY, LITTLE FLAME, JUST LIKE YOU WILL.

FIRST RULE OF TOA HUNTING: GET THEM ANGRY. IT MAKES THEM CARELESS. OVERCONFIDENCE MUST COME WITH THE KANOHI.

LIAR!

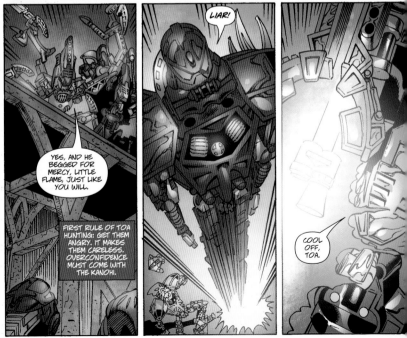

COOL OFF, TOA.

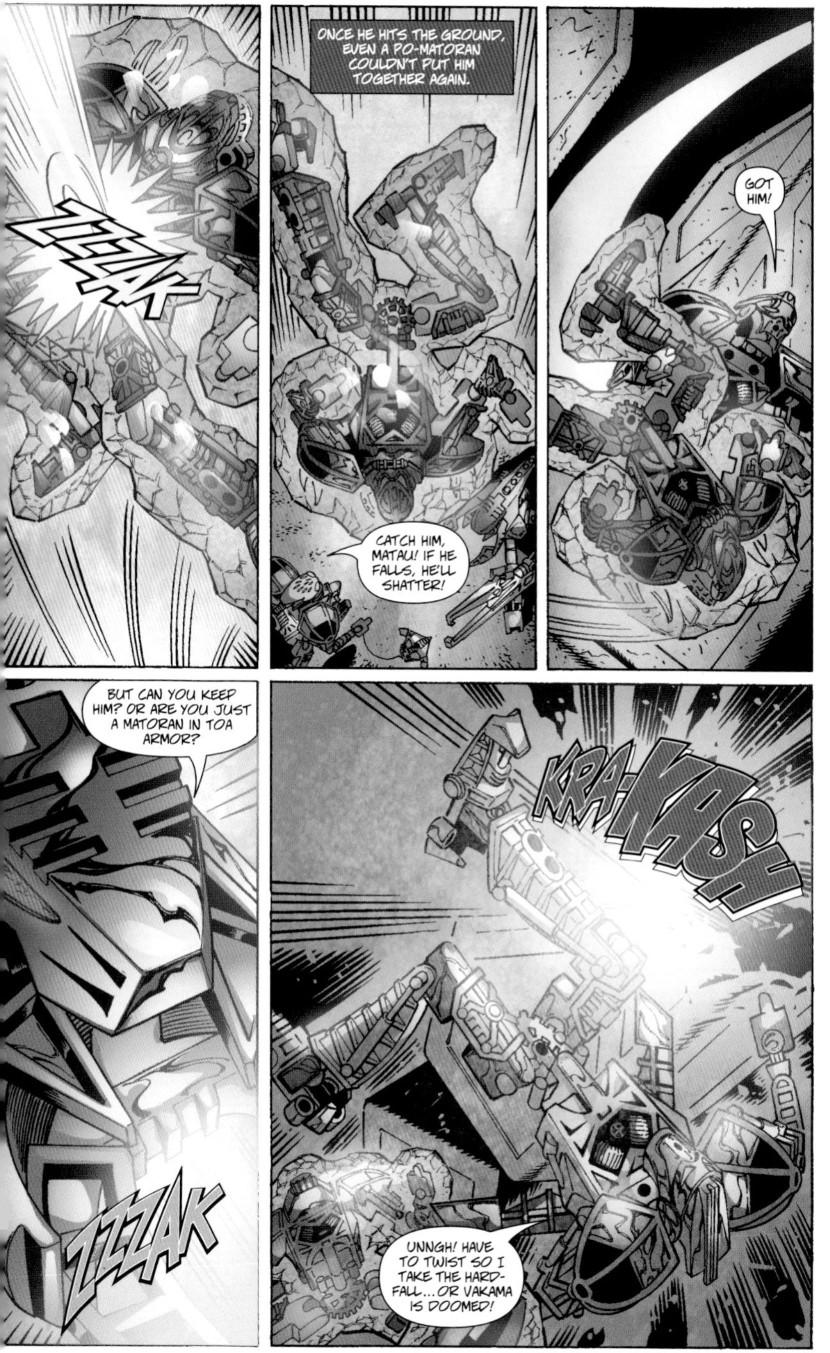
ZZZZAK
ONCE HE HITS THE GROUND, EVEN A PO-MATORAN COULDN'T PUT HIM TOGETHER AGAIN.
CATCH HIM, MATAU! IF HE FALLS, HE'LL SHATTER!
GOT HIM!
BUT CAN YOU KEEP HIM? OR ARE YOU JUST A MATORAN IN TOA ARMOR?
ZZZZAK
KRA-KASH
UNNGH! HAVE TO TWIST SO I TAKE THE HARD-FALL...OR VAKAMA IS DOOMED!

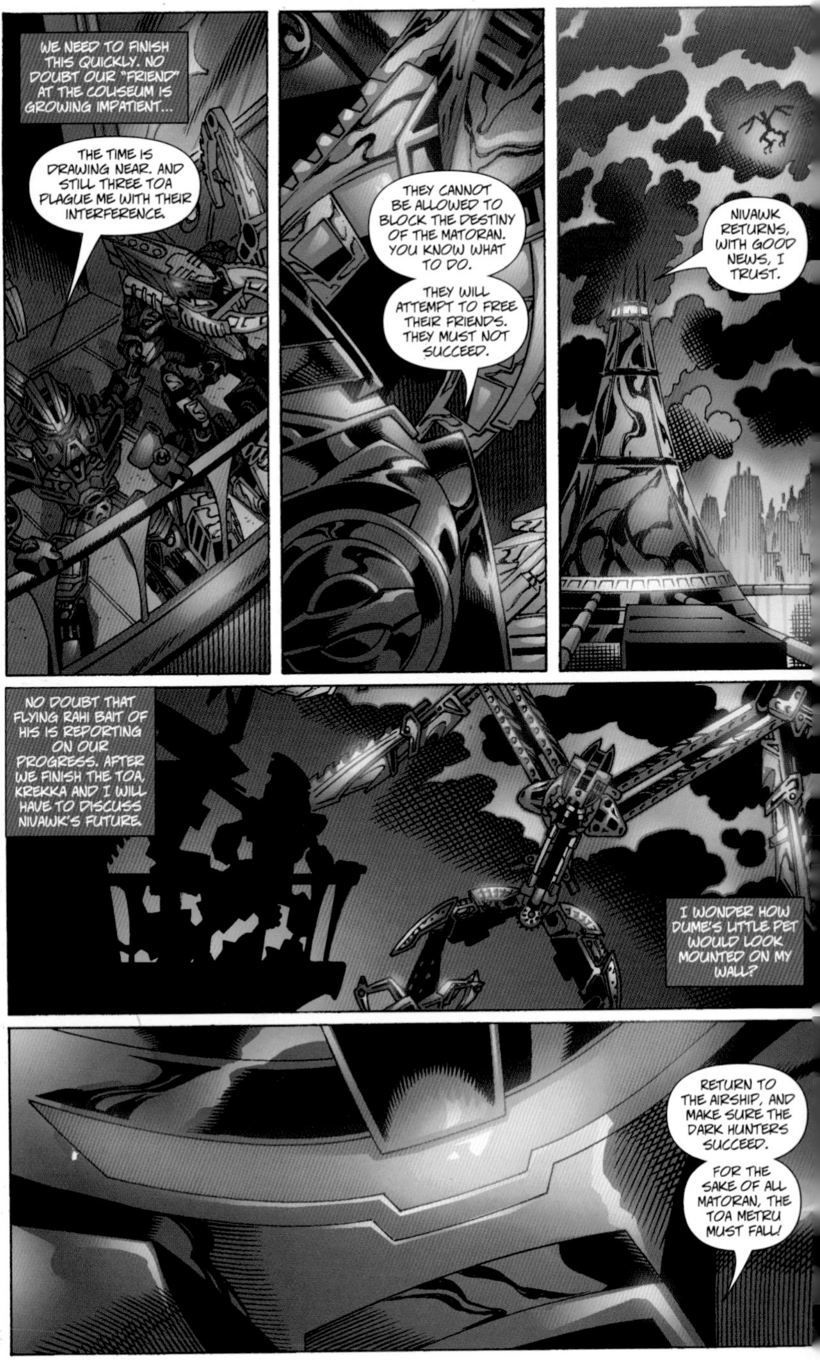
WE NEED TO FINISH THIS QUICKLY. NO DOUBT OUR "FRIEND" AT THE COLISEUM IS GROWING IMPATIENT...
THE TIME IS DRAWING NEAR. AND STILL THREE TOA PLAGUE ME WITH THEIR INTERFERENCE.
THEY CANNOT BE ALLOWED TO BLOCK THE DESTINY OF THE MATORAN. YOU KNOW WHAT TO DO.
THEY WILL ATTEMPT TO FREE THEIR FRIENDS. THEY MUST NOT SUCCEED.
NIVAWK RETURNS, WITH GOOD NEWS, I TRUST.
NO DOUBT THAT FLYING RAHI BAIT OF HIS IS REPORTING ON OUR PROGRESS. AFTER WE FINISH THE TOA, KREKKA AND I WILL HAVE TO DISCUSS NIVAWK'S FUTURE.
I WONDER HOW DUME'S LITTLE PET WOULD LOOK MOUNTED ON MY WALL?
RETURN TO THE AIRSHIP, AND MAKE SURE THE DARK HUNTERS SUCCEED.
FOR THE SAKE OF ALL MATORAN, THE TOA METRU MUST FALL!

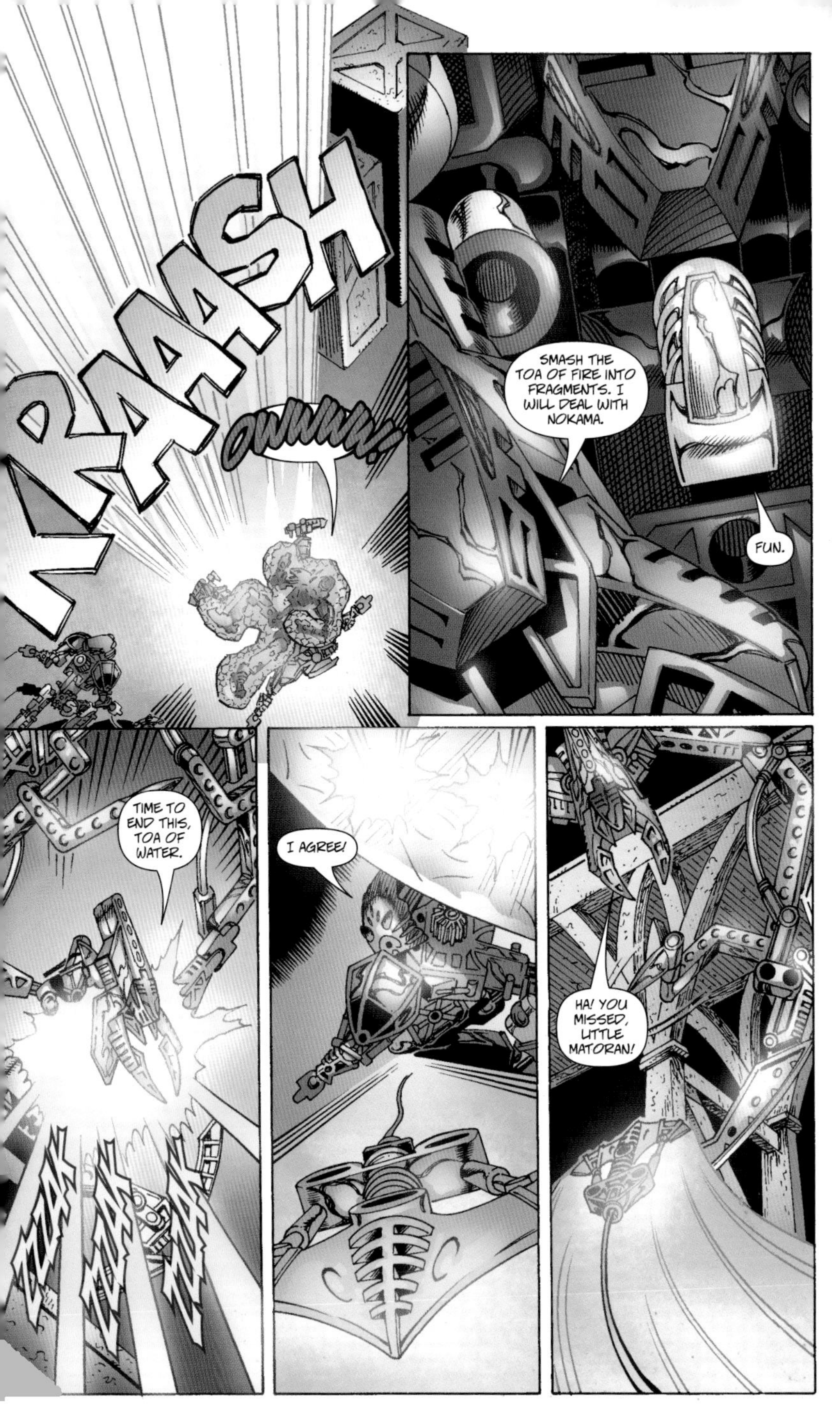
KRAASH
OWWWW!!
SMASH THE TOA OF FIRE INTO FRAGMENTS. I WILL DEAL WITH NOKAMA.
FUN.
TIME TO END THIS, TOA OF WATER.
I AGREE!
HA! YOU MISSED, LITTLE MATORAN!

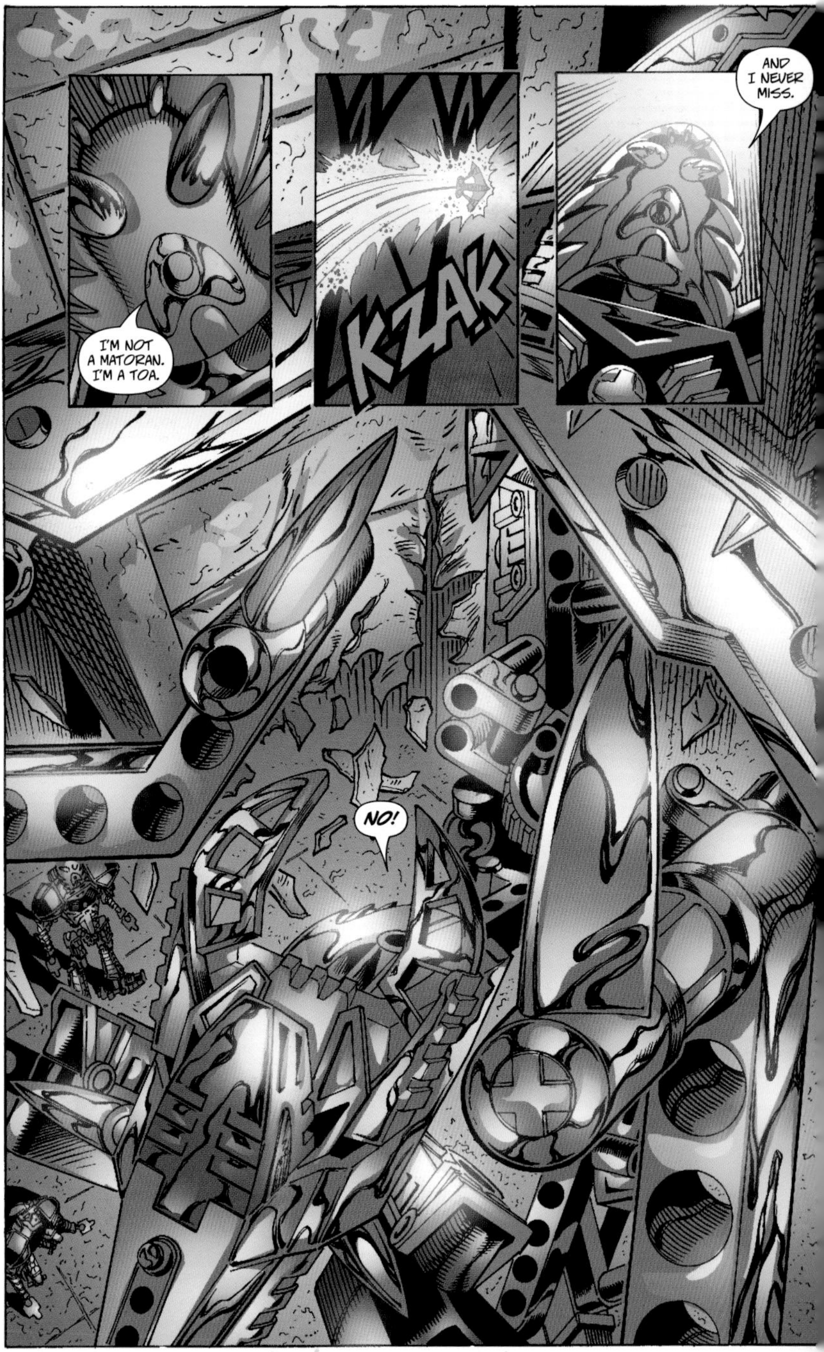
I'M NOT A MATORAN. I'M A TOA.
KZAK
AND I NEVER MISS.
NO!

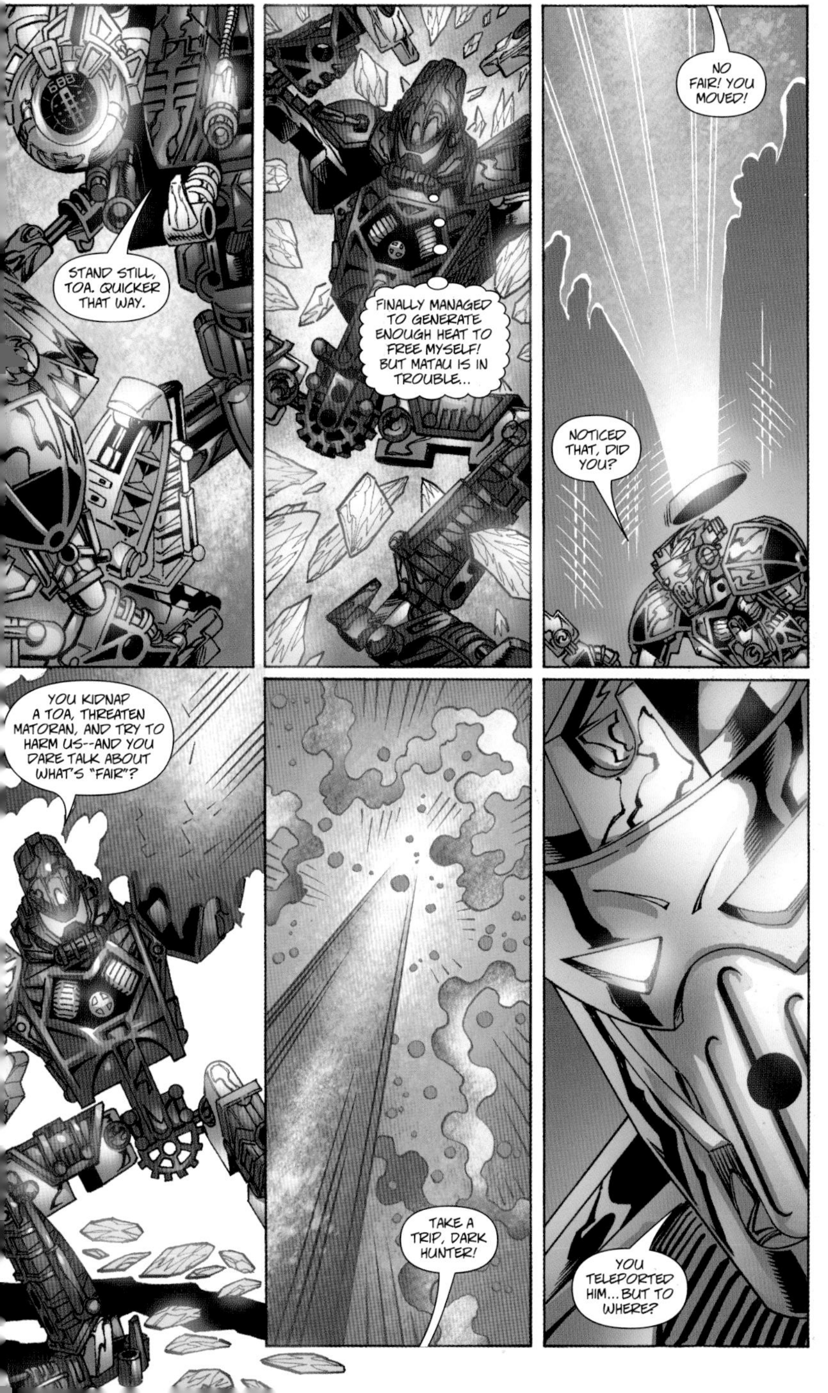
STAND STILL, TOA. QUICKER THAT WAY.
FINALLY MANAGED TO GENERATE ENOUGH HEAT TO FREE MYSELF! BUT MATAU IS IN TROUBLE...
NO FAIR! YOU MOVED!
NOTICED THAT, DID YOU?
YOU KIDNAP A TOA, THREATEN MATORAN, AND TRY TO HARM US--AND YOU DARE TALK ABOUT WHAT'S "FAIR"?
TAKE A TRIP, DARK HUNTER!
YOU TELEPORTED HIM... BUT TO WHERE?

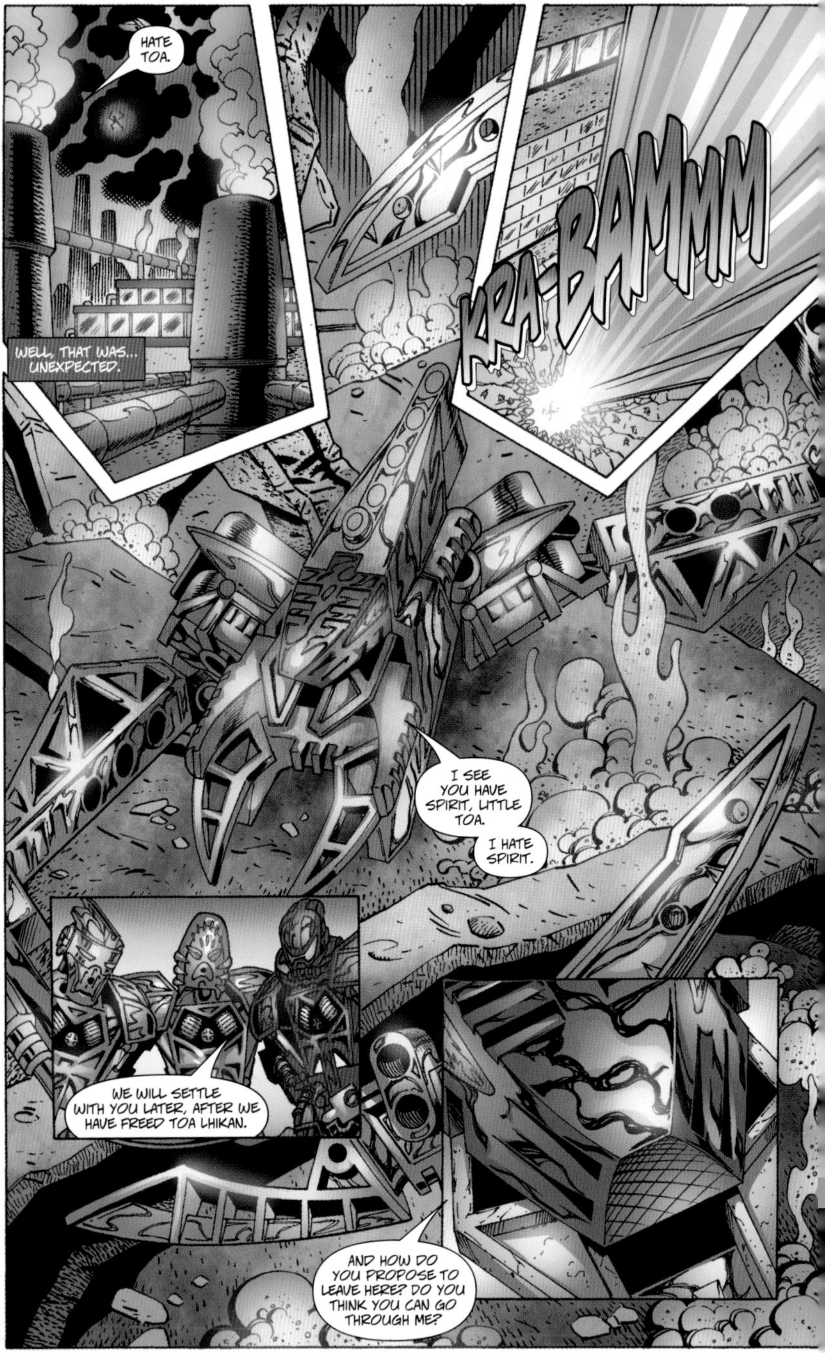
HATE TOA.
WELL, THAT WAS... UNEXPECTED.
KRA-BAMMM
I SEE YOU HAVE SPIRIT, LITTLE TOA.
I HATE SPIRIT.
WE WILL SETTLE WITH YOU LATER, AFTER WE HAVE FREED TOA LHIKAN.
AND HOW DO YOU PROPOSE TO LEAVE HERE? DO YOU THINK YOU CAN GO THROUGH ME?

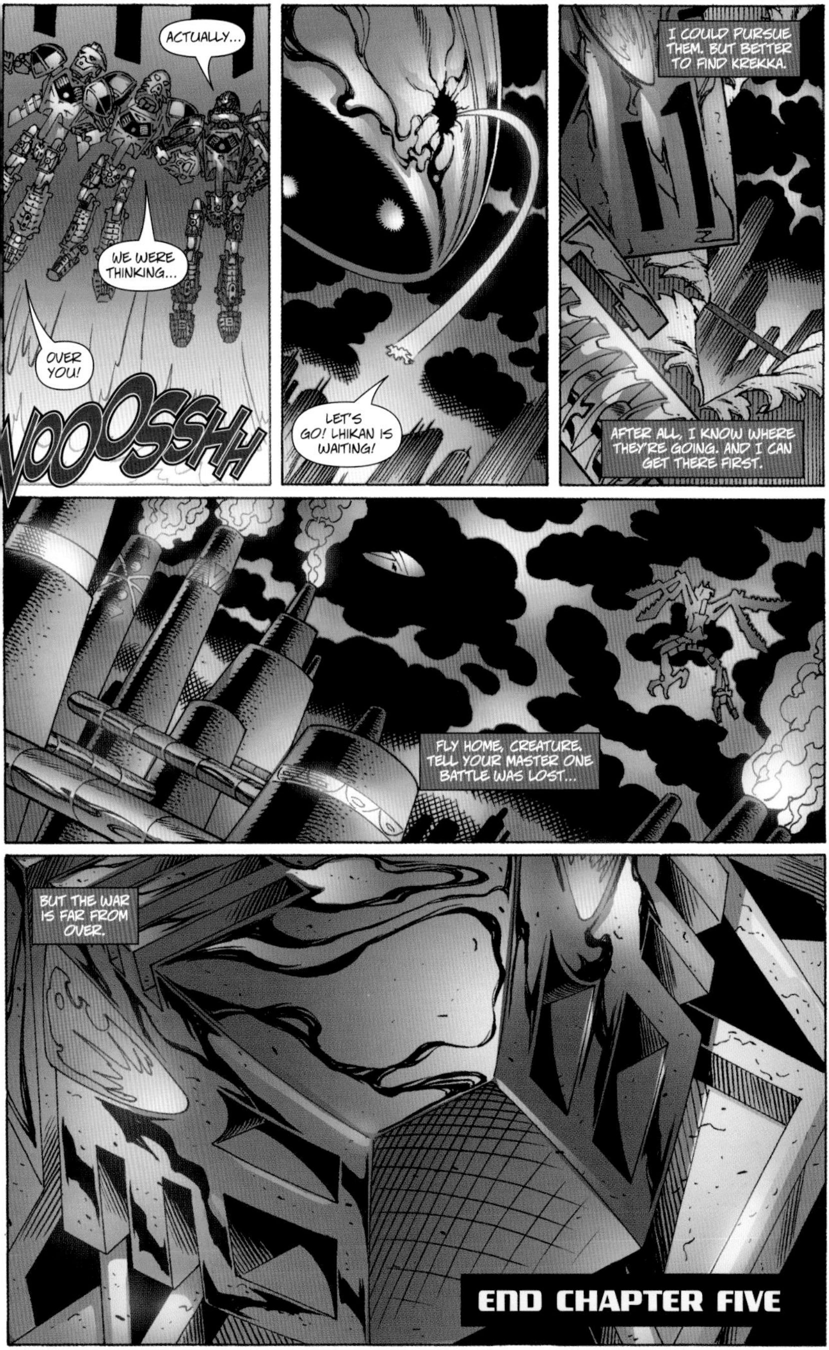
ACTUALLY...
WE WERE THINKING...
OVER YOU!
VOOOSSHH
LET'S GO! LHIKAN IS WAITING!
I COULD PURSUE THEM. BUT BETTER TO FIND KREKKA.
AFTER ALL, I KNOW WHERE THEY'RE GOING. AND I CAN GET THERE FIRST.
FLY HOME, CREATURE. TELL YOUR MASTER ONE BATTLE WAS LOST...
BUT THE WAR IS FAR FROM OVER.
END CHAPTER FIVE

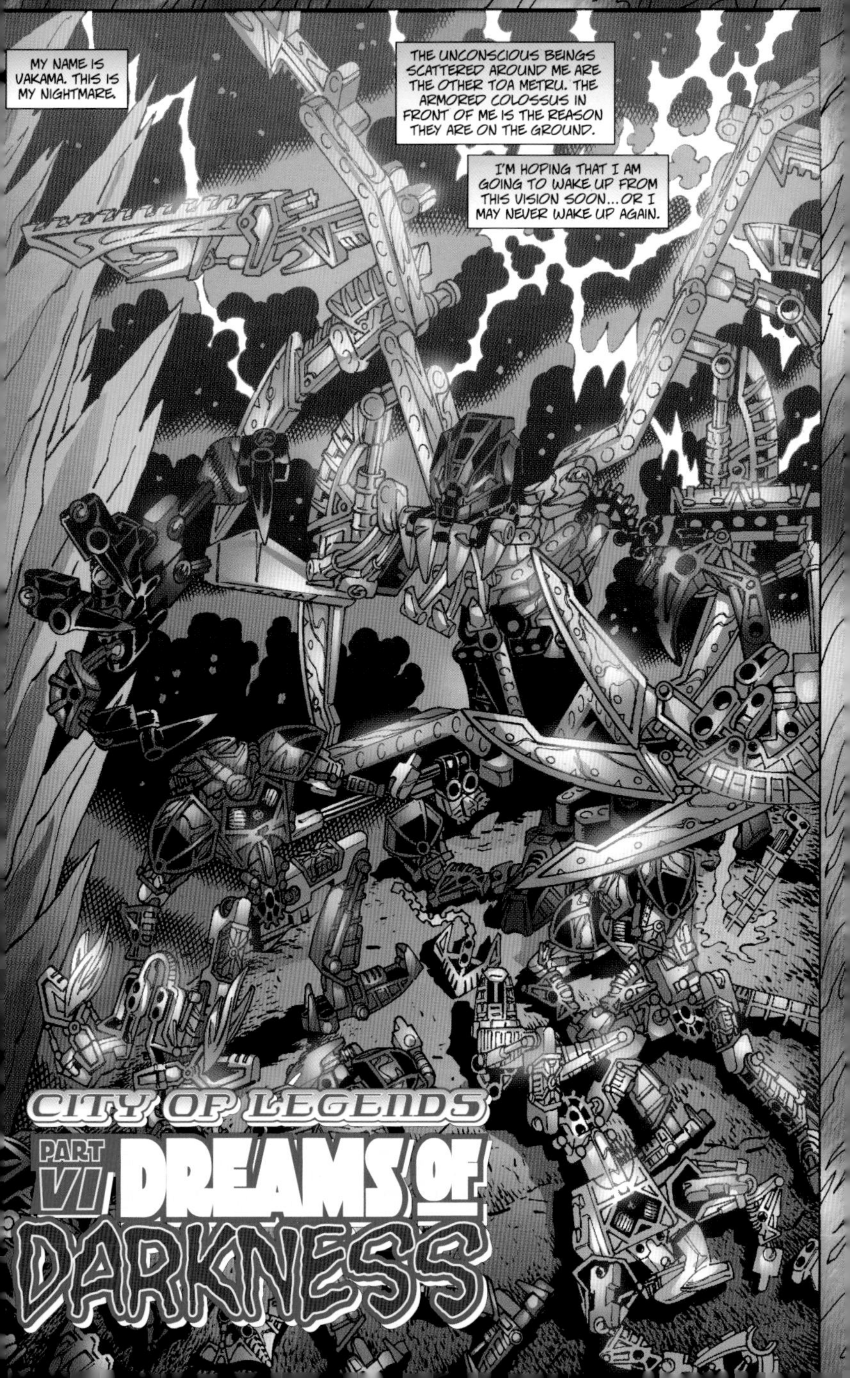
MY NAME IS VAKAMA. THIS IS MY NIGHTMARE.
THE UNCONSCIOUS BEINGS SCATTERED AROUND ME ARE THE OTHER TOA METRU. THE ARMORED COLOSSUS IN FRONT OF ME IS THE REASON THEY ARE ON THE GROUND.
I'M HOPING THAT I AM GOING TO WAKE UP FROM THIS VISION SOON...OR I MAY NEVER WAKE UP AGAIN.
CITY OF LEGENDS
PART VI DREAMS OF DARKNESS

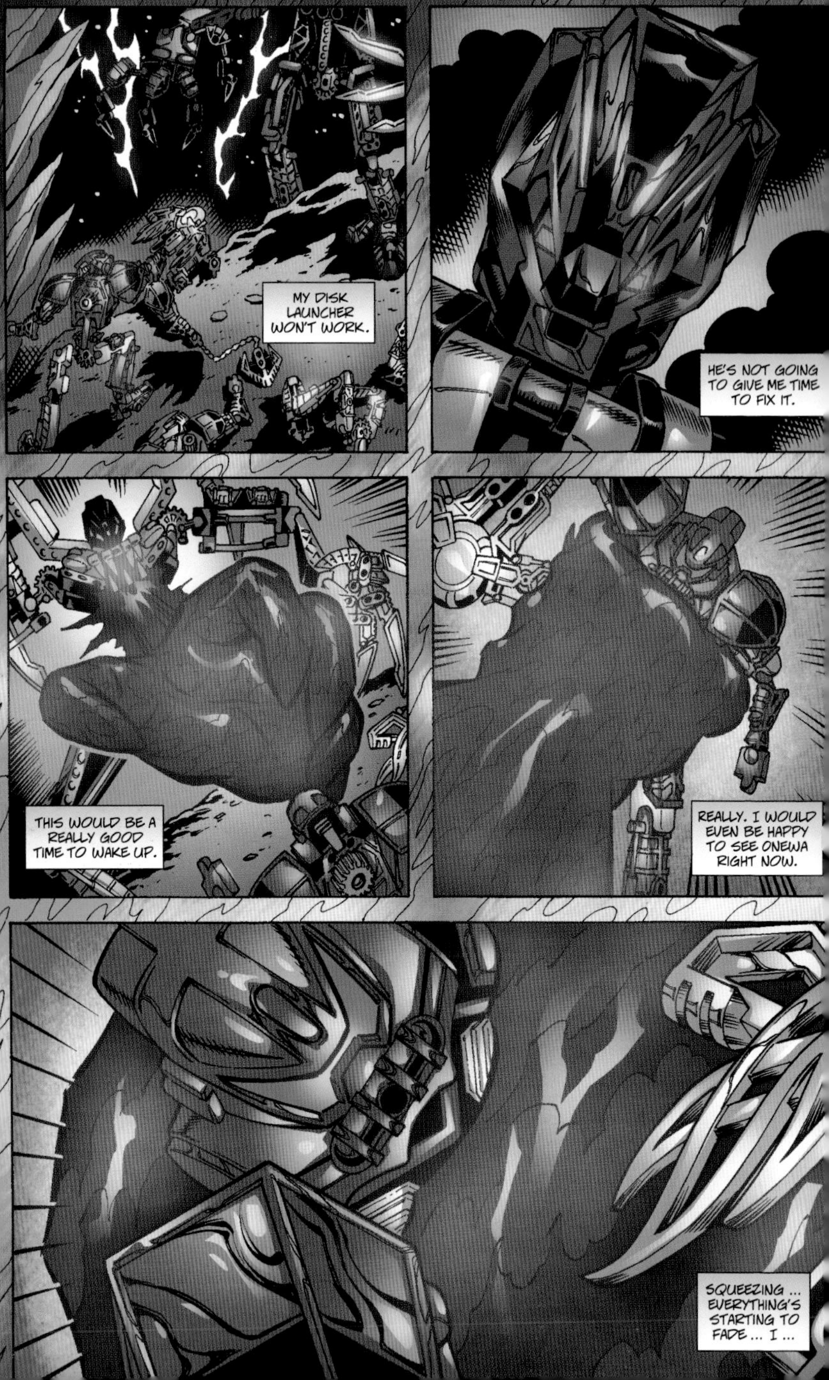
MY DISK LAUNCHER WON'T WORK.
HE'S NOT GOING TO GIVE ME TIME TO FIX IT.
THIS WOULD BE A REALLY GOOD TIME TO WAKE UP.
REALLY. I WOULD EVEN BE HAPPY TO SEE ONEWA RIGHT NOW.
SQUEEZING ... EVERYTHING'S STARTING TO FADE ... I ...

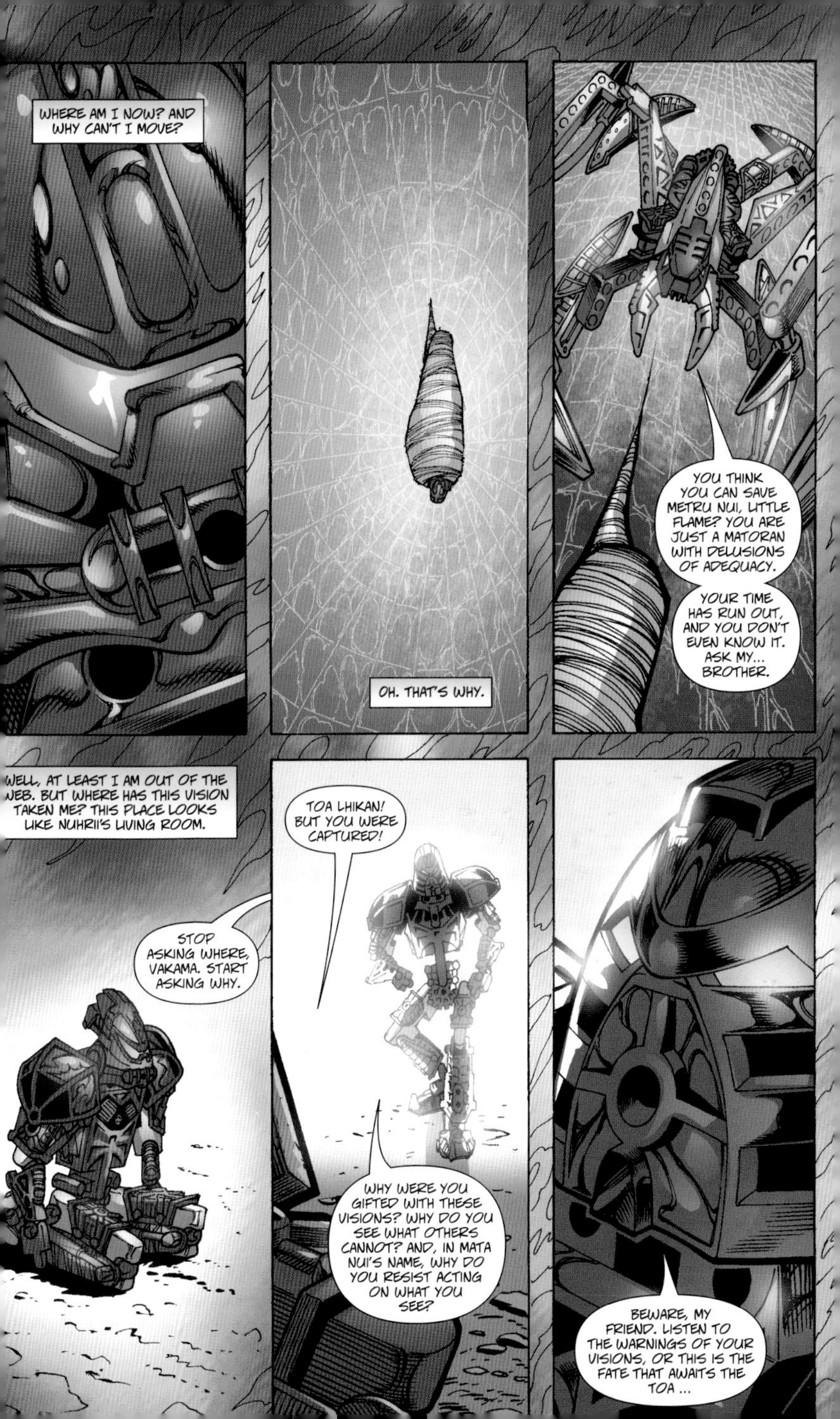
WHERE AM I NOW? AND WHY CAN'T I MOVE?
OH. THAT'S WHY.
YOU THINK YOU CAN SAVE METRU NUI, LITTLE FLAME? YOU ARE JUST A MATORAN WITH DELUSIONS OF ADEQUACY.
YOUR TIME HAS RUN OUT, AND YOU DON'T EVEN KNOW IT. ASK MY... BROTHER.
WELL, AT LEAST I AM OUT OF THE WEB. BUT WHERE HAS THIS VISION TAKEN ME? THIS PLACE LOOKS LIKE NUHRII'S LIVING ROOM.
TOA LHIKAN! BUT YOU WERE CAPTURED!
STOP ASKING WHERE, VAKAMA. START ASKING WHY.
WHY WERE YOU GIFTED WITH THESE VISIONS? WHY DO YOU SEE WHAT OTHERS CANNOT? AND, IN MATA NUI'S NAME, WHY DO YOU RESIST ACTING ON WHAT YOU SEE?
BEWARE, MY FRIEND. LISTEN TO THE WARNINGS OF YOUR VISIONS, OR THIS IS THE FATE THAT AWAITS THE TOA ...

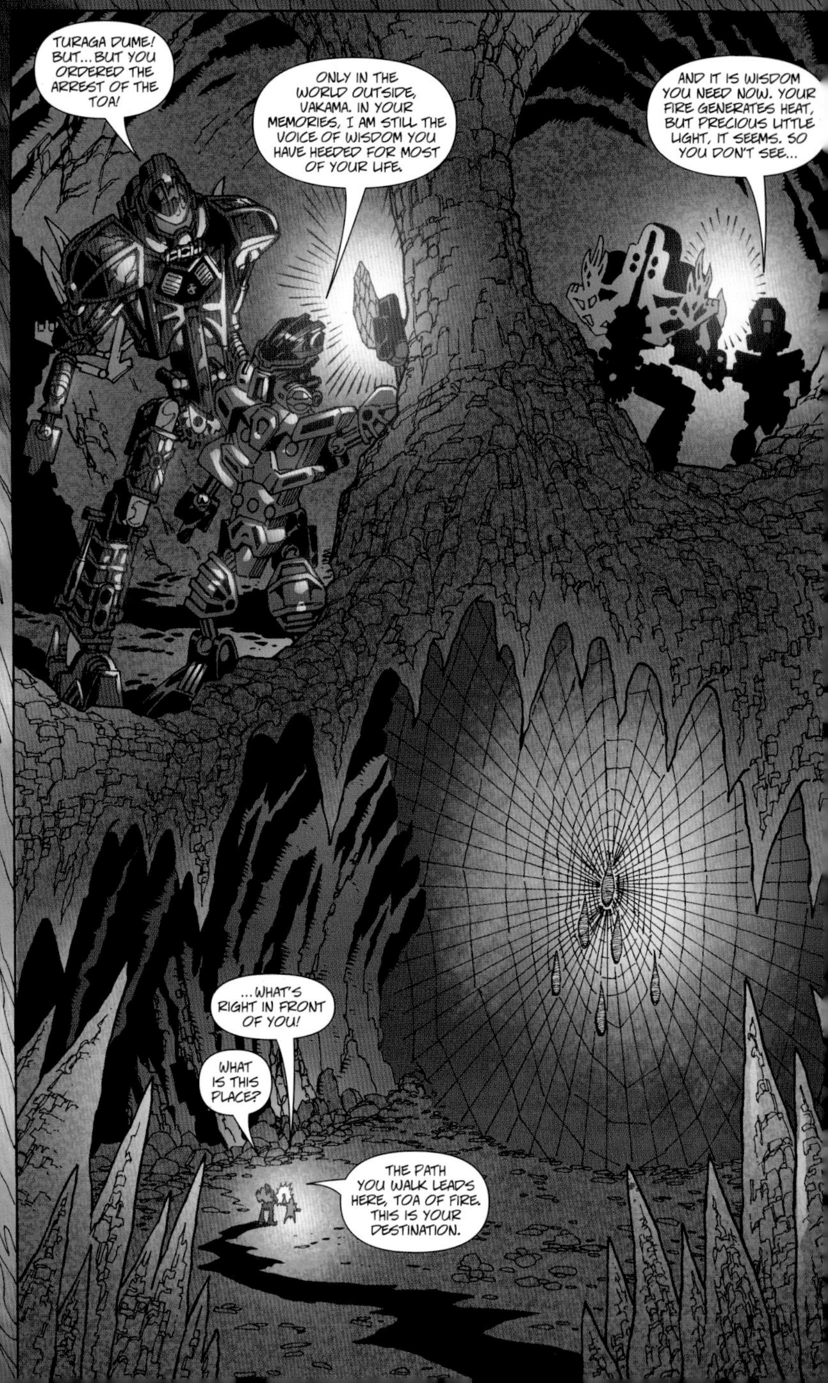
TURAGA DUME! BUT... BUT YOU ORDERED THE ARREST OF THE TOA!
ONLY IN THE WORLD OUTSIDE, VAKAMA. IN YOUR MEMORIES, I AM STILL THE VOICE OF WISDOM YOU HAVE HEEDED FOR MOST OF YOUR LIFE.
AND IT IS WISDOM YOU NEED NOW. YOUR FIRE GENERATES HEAT, BUT PRECIOUS LITTLE LIGHT, IT SEEMS. SO YOU DON'T SEE...
...WHAT'S RIGHT IN FRONT OF YOU!
WHAT IS THIS PLACE?
THE PATH YOU WALK LEADS HERE, TOA OF FIRE. THIS IS YOUR DESTINATION.

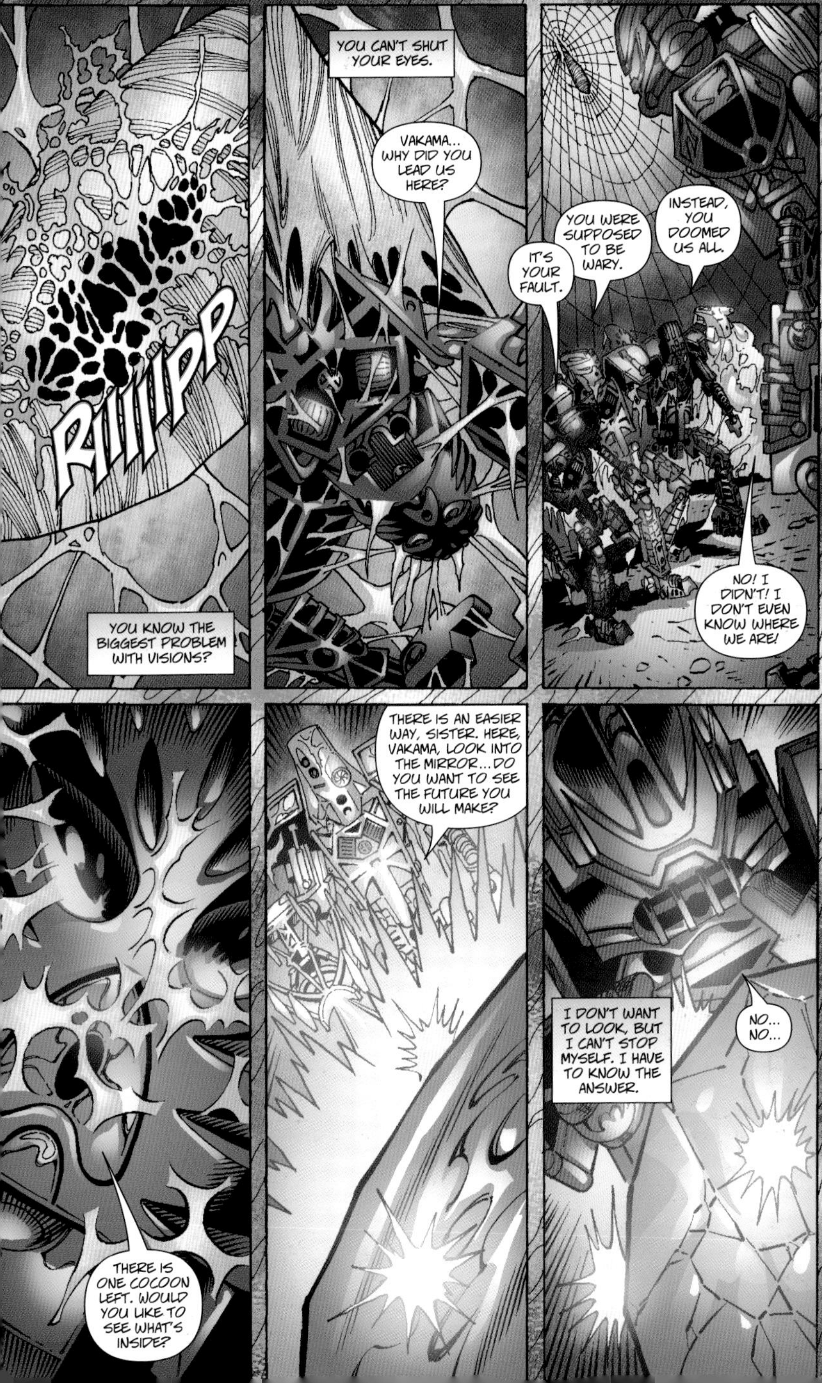
RIIIIPP
YOU KNOW THE BIGGEST PROBLEM WITH VISIONS?
YOU CAN'T SHUT YOUR EYES.
VAKAMA... WHY DID YOU LEAD US HERE?
IT'S YOUR FAULT.
YOU WERE SUPPOSED TO BE WARY.
INSTEAD, YOU DOOMED US ALL.
NO! I DIDN'T! I DON'T EVEN KNOW WHERE WE ARE!
THERE IS ONE COCOON LEFT. WOULD YOU LIKE TO SEE WHAT'S INSIDE?
THERE IS AN EASIER WAY, SISTER. HERE, VAKAMA, LOOK INTO THE MIRROR... DO YOU WANT TO SEE THE FUTURE YOU WILL MAKE?
I DON'T WANT TO LOOK, BUT I CAN'T STOP MYSELF. I HAVE TO KNOW THE ANSWER.
NO... NO...

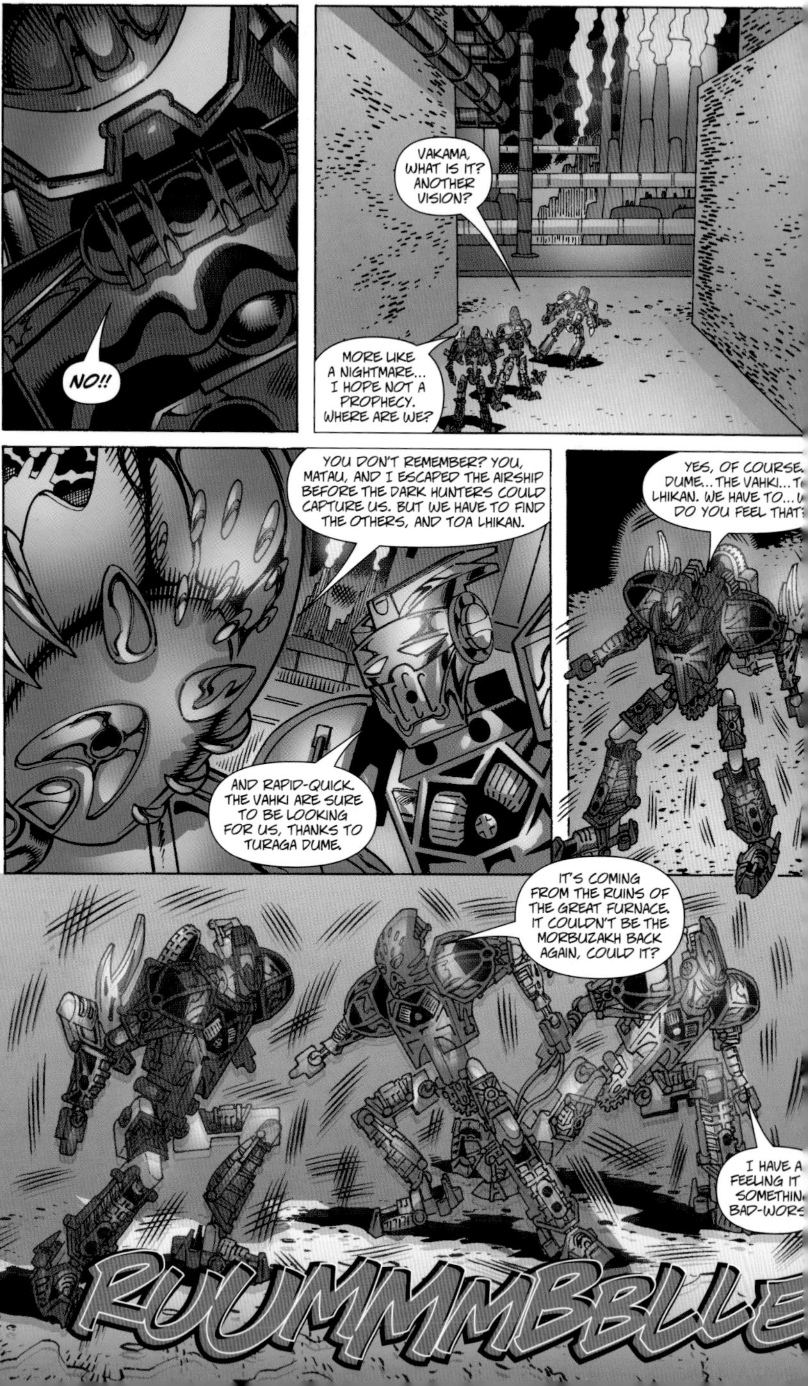
NO!!
VAKAMA, WHAT IS IT? ANOTHER VISION?
MORE LIKE A NIGHTMARE... I HOPE NOT A PROPHECY. WHERE ARE WE?
YOU DON'T REMEMBER? YOU, MATAU, AND I ESCAPED THE AIRSHIP BEFORE THE DARK HUNTERS COULD CAPTURE US. BUT WE HAVE TO FIND THE OTHERS, AND TOA LHIKAN.
AND RAPID-QUICK. THE VAHKI ARE SURE TO BE LOOKING FOR US, THANKS TO TURAGA DUME.
YES, OF COURSE. DUME... THE VAHKI... LHIKAN. WE HAVE TO... DO YOU FEEL THAT
IT'S COMING FROM THE RUINS OF THE GREAT FURNACE. IT COULDN'T BE THE MORBUZAKH BACK AGAIN, COULD IT?
I HAVE A FEELING IT SOMETHIN BAD-WORS
RUUMMMBBLLE

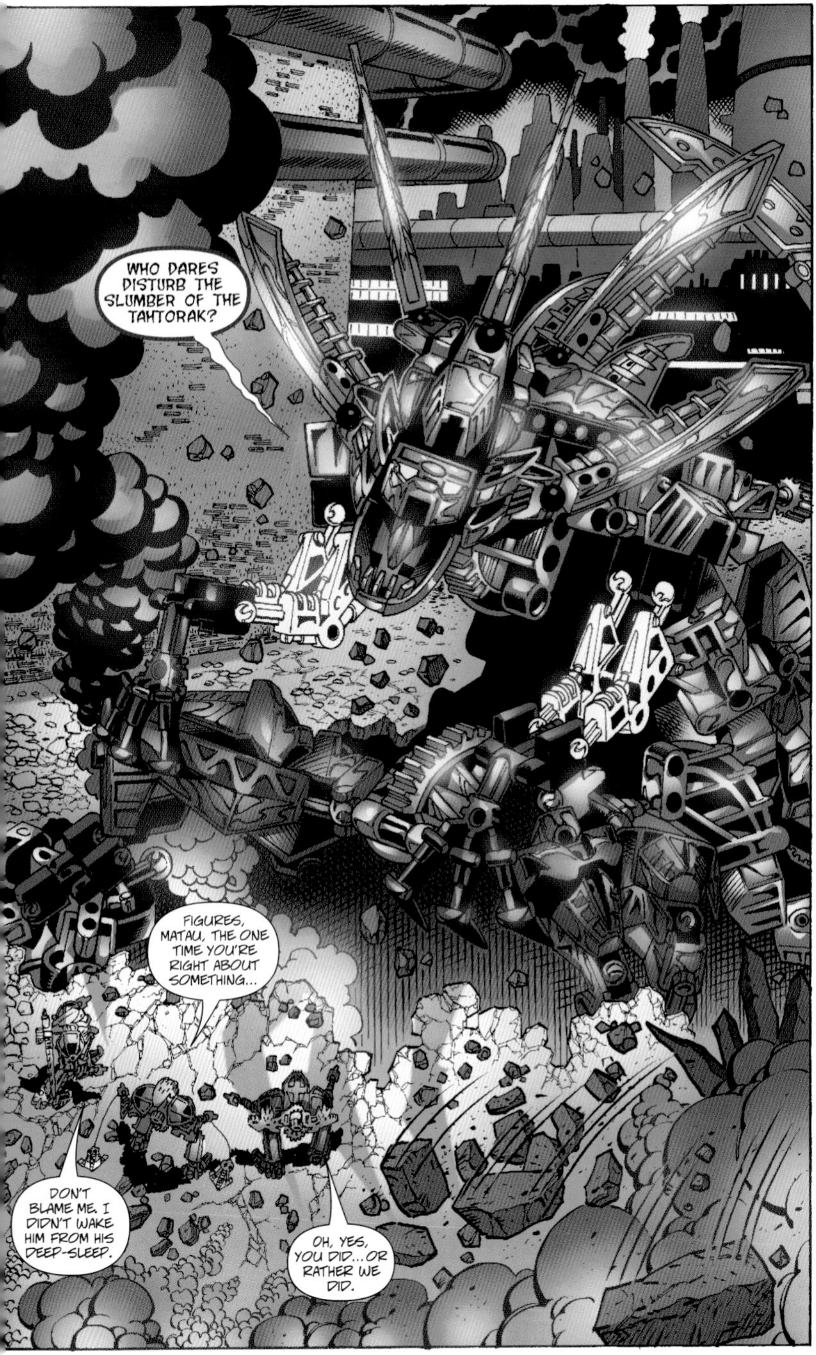
WHO DARES DISTURB THE SLUMBER OF THE TAHTORAK?
FIGURES, MATAU, THE ONE TIME YOU'RE RIGHT ABOUT SOMETHING...
DON'T BLAME ME. I DIDN'T WAKE HIM FROM HIS DEEP-SLEEP.
OH, YES, YOU DID... OR RATHER WE DID.

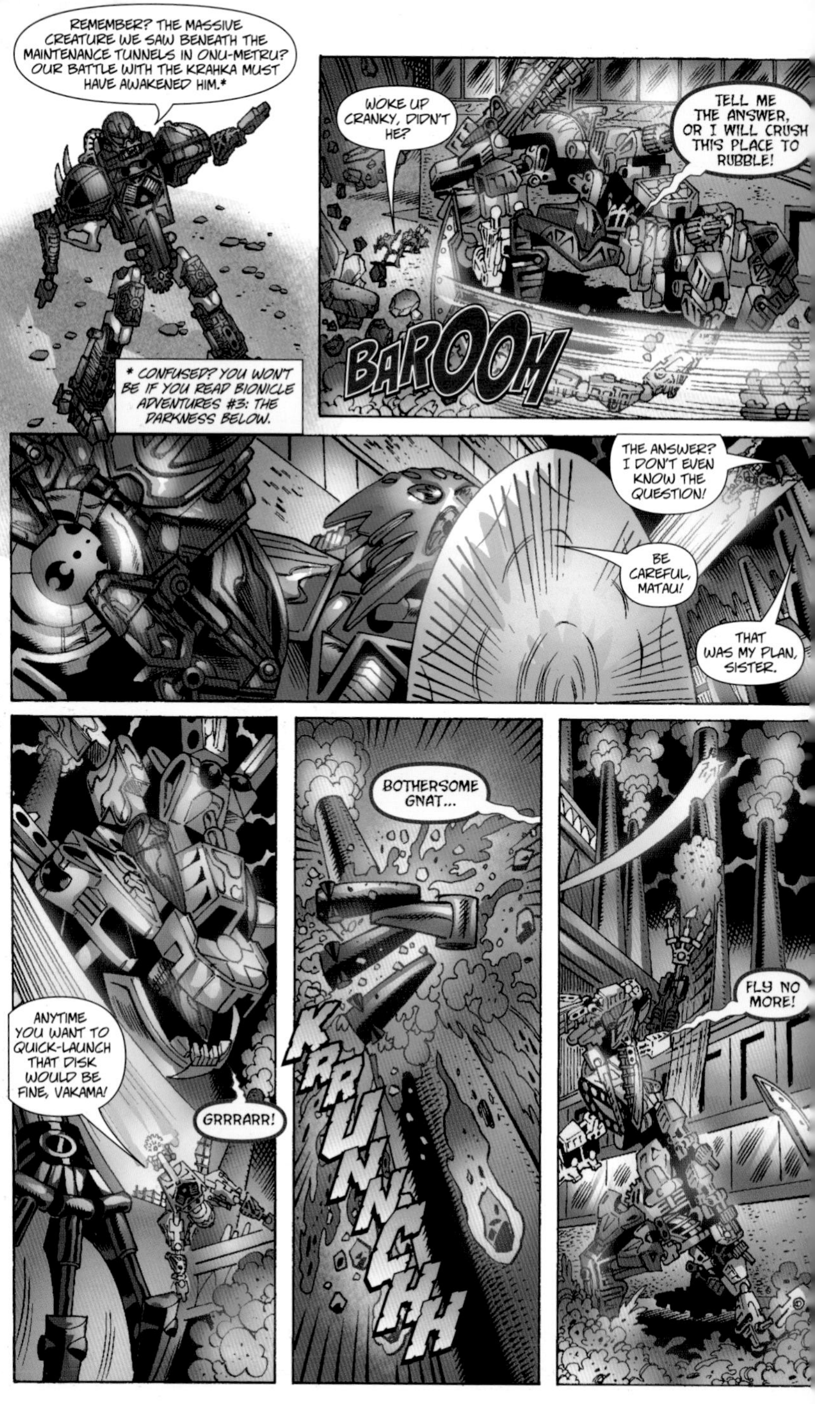
REMEMBER? THE MASSIVE CREATURE WE SAW BENEATH THE MAINTENANCE TUNNELS IN ONU-METRU? OUR BATTLE WITH THE KRAHKA MUST HAVE AWAKENED HIM.*
* CONFUSED? YOU WON'T BE IF YOU READ BIONICLE ADVENTURES #3: THE DARKNESS BELOW.
WOKE UP CRANKY, DIDN'T HE?
TELL ME THE ANSWER, OR I WILL CRUSH THIS PLACE TO RUBBLE!
BAROOOM
THE ANSWER? I DON'T EVEN KNOW THE QUESTION!
BE CAREFUL, MATAU!
THAT WAS MY PLAN, SISTER.
ANYTIME YOU WANT TO QUICK-LAUNCH THAT DISK WOULD BE FINE, VAKAMA!
GRRRARR!
BOTHERSOME GNAT...
KRRUNNCHH
FLY NO MORE!

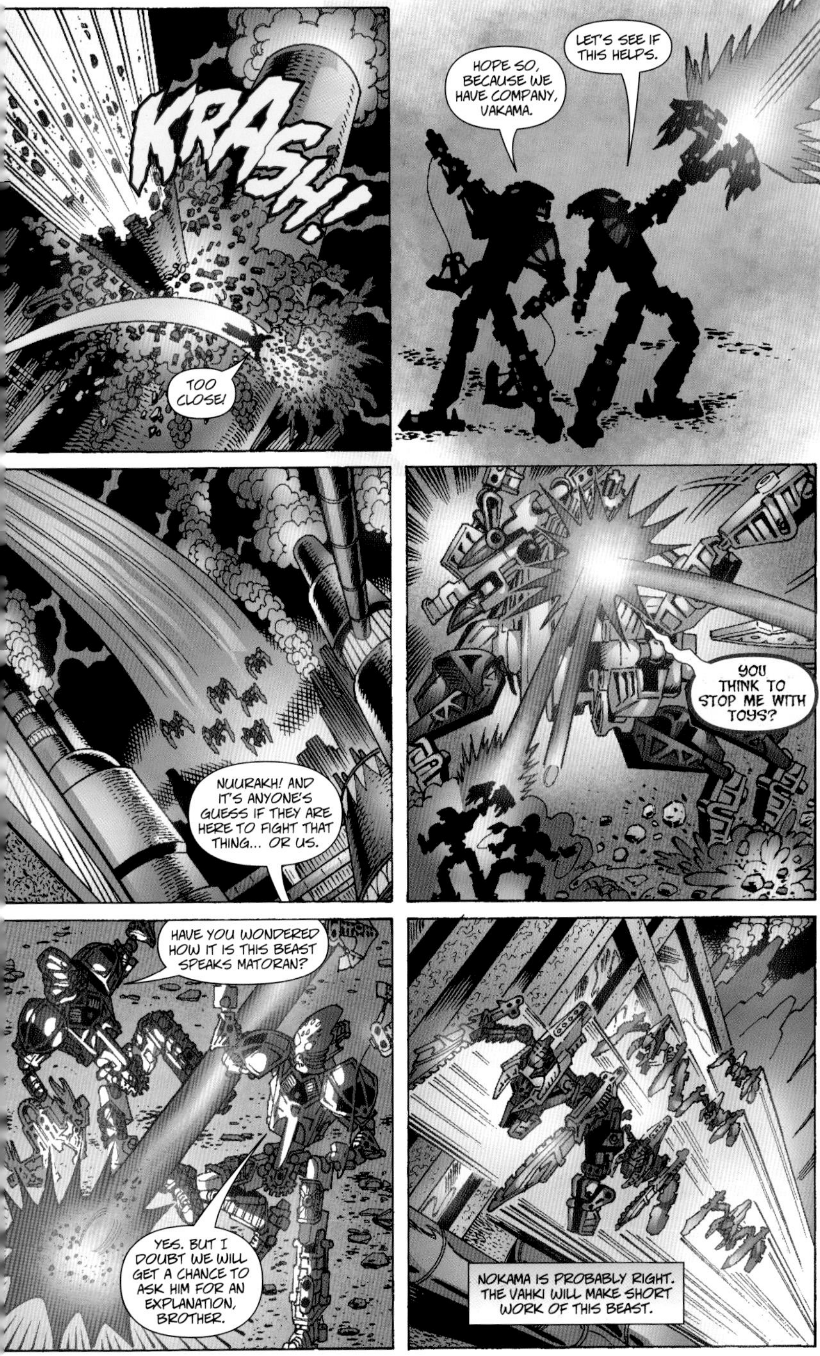
KRASH!
TOO CLOSE!
HOPE SO, BECAUSE WE HAVE COMPANY, VAKAMA.
LET'S SEE IF THIS HELPS.
NUURAKH! AND IT'S ANYONE'S GUESS IF THEY ARE HERE TO FIGHT THAT THING... OR US.
YOU THINK TO STOP ME WITH TOYS?
HAVE YOU WONDERED HOW IT IS THIS BEAST SPEAKS MATORAN?
YES. BUT I DOUBT WE WILL GET A CHANCE TO ASK HIM FOR AN EXPLANATION, BROTHER.
NOKAMA IS PROBABLY RIGHT. THE VAHKI WILL MAKE SHORT WORK OF THIS BEAST.

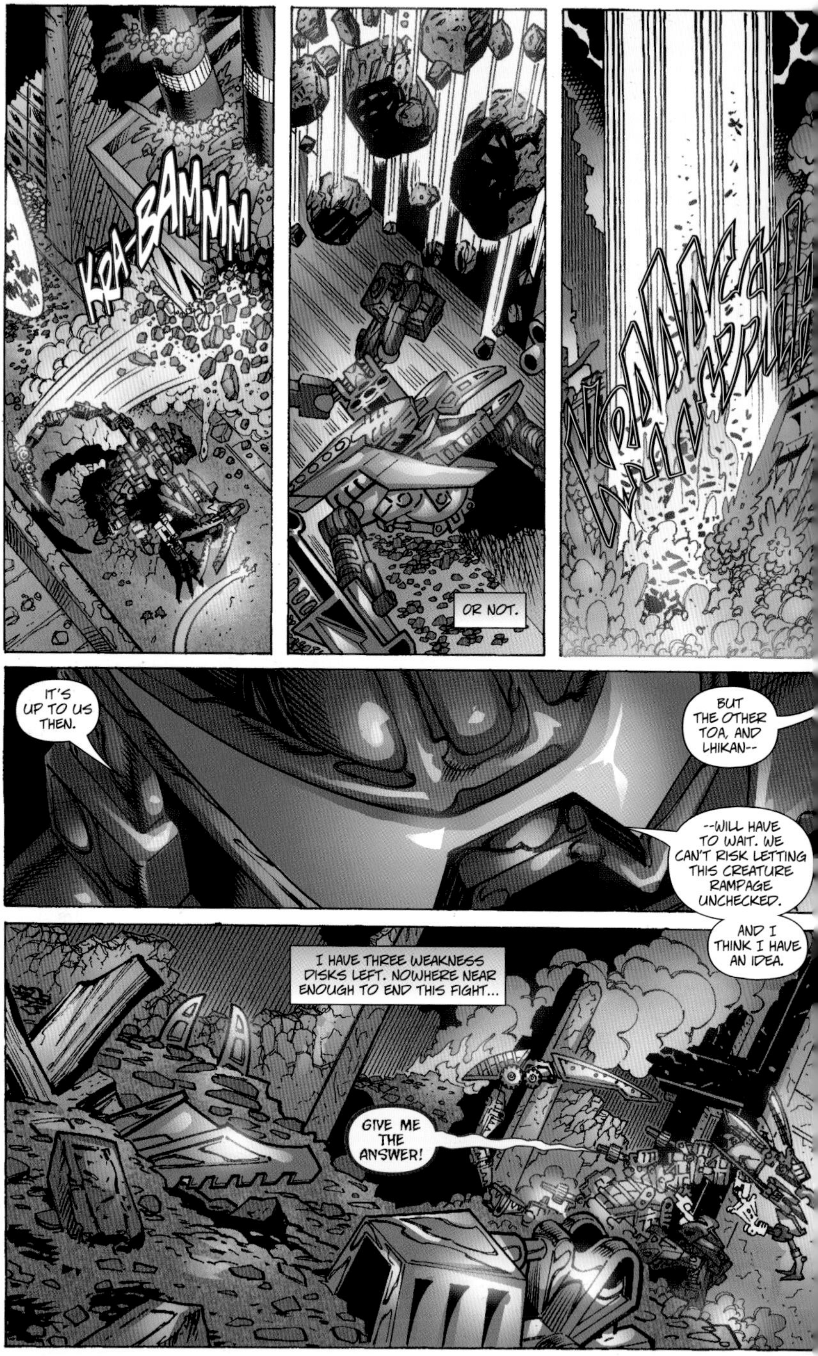
KRA-BAMMM
OR NOT.
IT'S UP TO US THEN.
BUT THE OTHER TOA, AND LHIKAN--
--WILL HAVE TO WAIT. WE CAN'T RISK LETTING THIS CREATURE RAMPAGE UNCHECKED.
AND I THINK I HAVE AN IDEA.
I HAVE THREE WEAKNESS DISKS LEFT. NOWHERE NEAR ENOUGH TO END THIS FIGHT...
GIVE ME THE ANSWER!

...IF WE WERE AIMING AT *HIM*.

THIS MAY NOT BE *THE* ANSWER, BUT IT'S THE ONLY ONE WE HAVE. NOW!

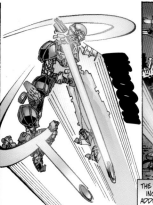

KLANG

THE TAHTORAK IS INCREDIBLY POWERFUL... AND INCREDIBLY HEAVY. WITH THE DISKS' POWER ADDED TO THE DAMAGE HE'S ALREADY DONE...

WHAT MADNESS--?

THE ANSWER! TELL ME THE ANSWER!

KRRACOOM

HE IS STILL FALLING, THROUGH LEVEL AFTER LEVEL. IS HE GONE FOR GOOD?

HE'S GONE FOR NOW. THAT HAS TO DO.

IT'S TIME WE WERE GONE TOO, BEFORE MORE VAHKI SHOW UP.

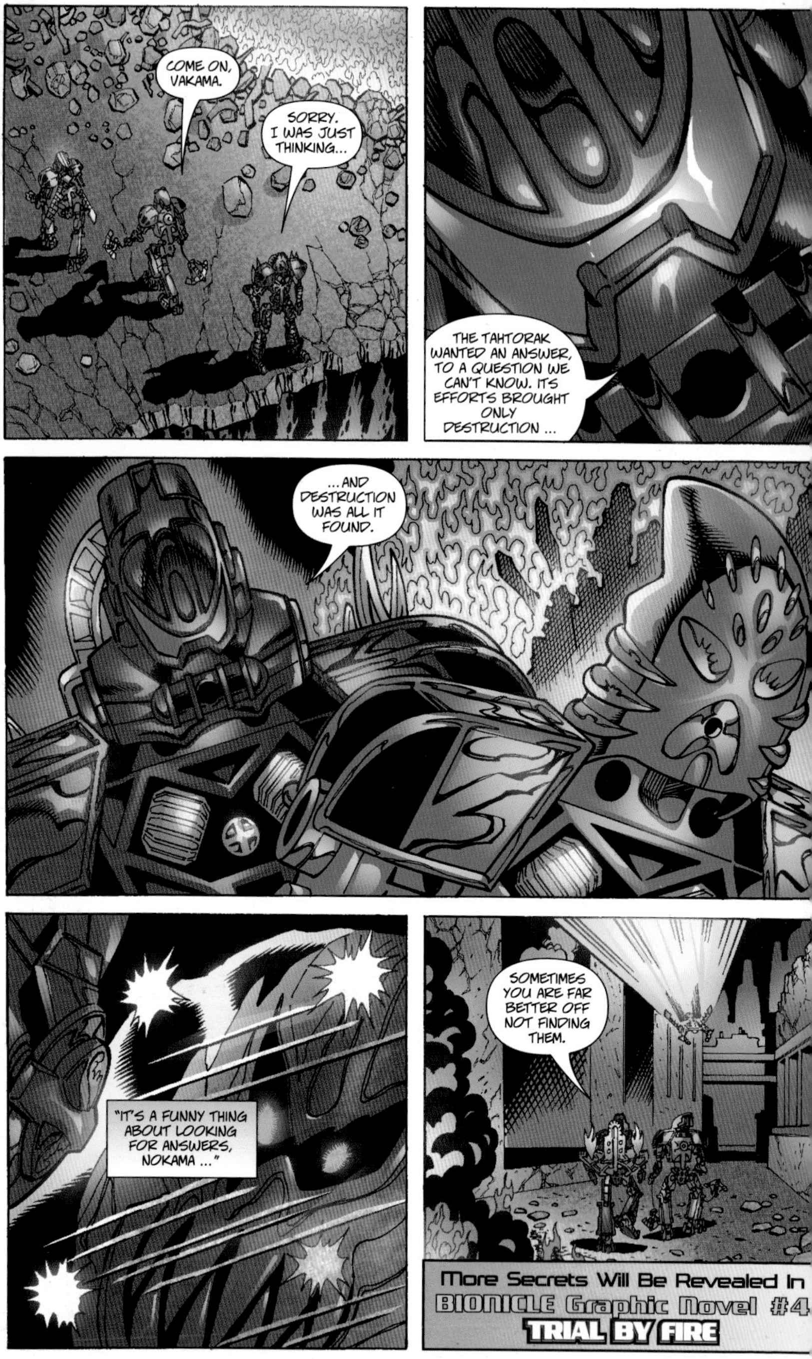
COME ON, VAKAMA.
SORRY. I WAS JUST THINKING...
THE TAHTORAK WANTED AN ANSWER, TO A QUESTION WE CAN'T KNOW. ITS EFFORTS BROUGHT ONLY DESTRUCTION ...
...AND DESTRUCTION WAS ALL IT FOUND.
"IT'S A FUNNY THING ABOUT LOOKING FOR ANSWERS, NOKAMA ..."
SOMETIMES YOU ARE FAR BETTER OFF NOT FINDING THEM.
More Secrets Will Be Revealed In
BIONICLE Graphic Novel #4
TRIAL BY FIRE

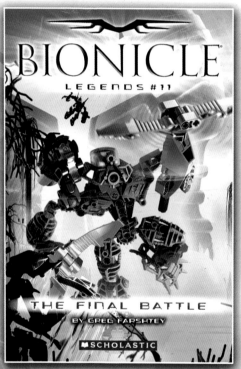

SECRETS of the KANOKA DISKS

When a **MATORAN** has to choose the right **KANOKA DISK** to defend his **METRU**, he looks at the disk code. But what do these codes mean? What powers do the **KANOKA DISKS** have, and how do **MATORAN** disk collectors know when they have stumbled on the rarest and most powerful ones? Read on!

The first digit identifies in which metru the disk was made. The metru of origin determines how the disk flies. "1" = Ta-Metru, "2" = Ga-Metru, "3" = Onu-Metru, "4" = Po-Metru, "5" = Le-Metru and "6" = Ko-Metru.

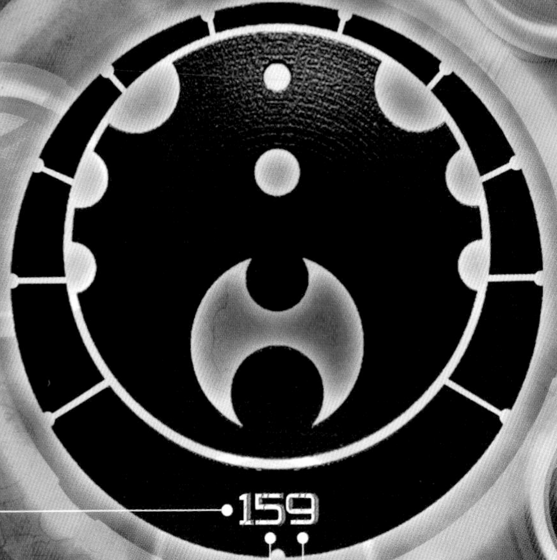
159

The second digit identifies the power of the disk. "1" = reconstitutes at random, "2" = freeze, "3" = weaken, "4" = remove poison, "5" = enlarge, "6" = shrink, "7" = regenerate and "8" = teleport.

The third digit identifies the power level of the disk. Power levels go from 1 to 9, with 9 being the highest.

THE HARDY BOYS®

NEW GRAPHIC NOVEL EVERY 3 MONTHS!

0 – "A Hardy Day's Night"
3N – 978-1-59707-070-6
1 – "Abracadeath"
3N – 978-1-59707-080-5
2 – "Dude Ranch O' Death!"
3N – 978-1-59707-088-1
3 – "The Deadliest Stunt"
3N – 978-1-59707-102-4
EW! #14 – "Haley Danelle's Top Eight!"
3N – 978-1-59707-113-0
so available – Hardy Boys #1-9
: Pocket sized, 96-112pp., full-color, $7.95
so available in hardcover! $12.95 each.

ON SALE NOW!

NEW STORY! FULL-COLOR GRAPHIC NOVEL
THE HARDY BOYS®
#14
HALEY DANELLE'S TOP EIGHT
based on the series by Franklin W. Dixon
UNDERCOVER BROTHERS™
Scott LOBDELL
Paulo HENRIQUE
PAPERCUTZ

IE HARDY BOYS
-4 Box Set
7 1/2, 400 pages, full-color, $29.95
3N – 978-1-59707-040-9
-8 Box Set
7 1/2, 432 pages, full-color, $29.95
3N – 978-1-59707-075-1
-12 Box Set
7 1/2, 448 pages, full-color, $29.95
3N - 978-1-59707-125-0

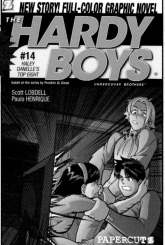

CLASSICS *Illustrated*®

Featuring Stories by the World's Greatest Authors

1 "Great Expectations"
BN – 978-1-59707-097-3
2 "The Invisible Man"
BN – 978-1-59707-106-2
EW! #3 "Through the Looking Glass"
BN – 978-1-59707-115-4
: 6 1/2 x 9, 56 pages, full-color

FULL-COLOR GRAPHIC NOVEL ADAPTATION
CLASSICS Illustrated®
Featuring Stories by the World's Greatest Authors
THROUGH THE LOOKING-GLASS
By Lewis Carroll
Adapted by
PAPERCUTZ

At bookstores or order at Papercutz, 40 Exchange Place, Ste. 1308, New York, NY 10005, 1-800-886-1223 (M-F 9-6 EST) Please add $4.00 postage and handling, $1 each additional item. Make check payable to NBM publishing. MC, VISA, AMEX accepted, Distributed by Macmillan

PAPERCUTZ™.COM

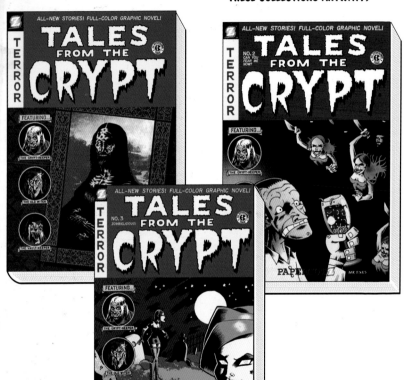

Have you discovered the Hardy Boys Graphic Novels yet?
Here's a preview from VOLUME #15: "Live Free, Die Hardy!"

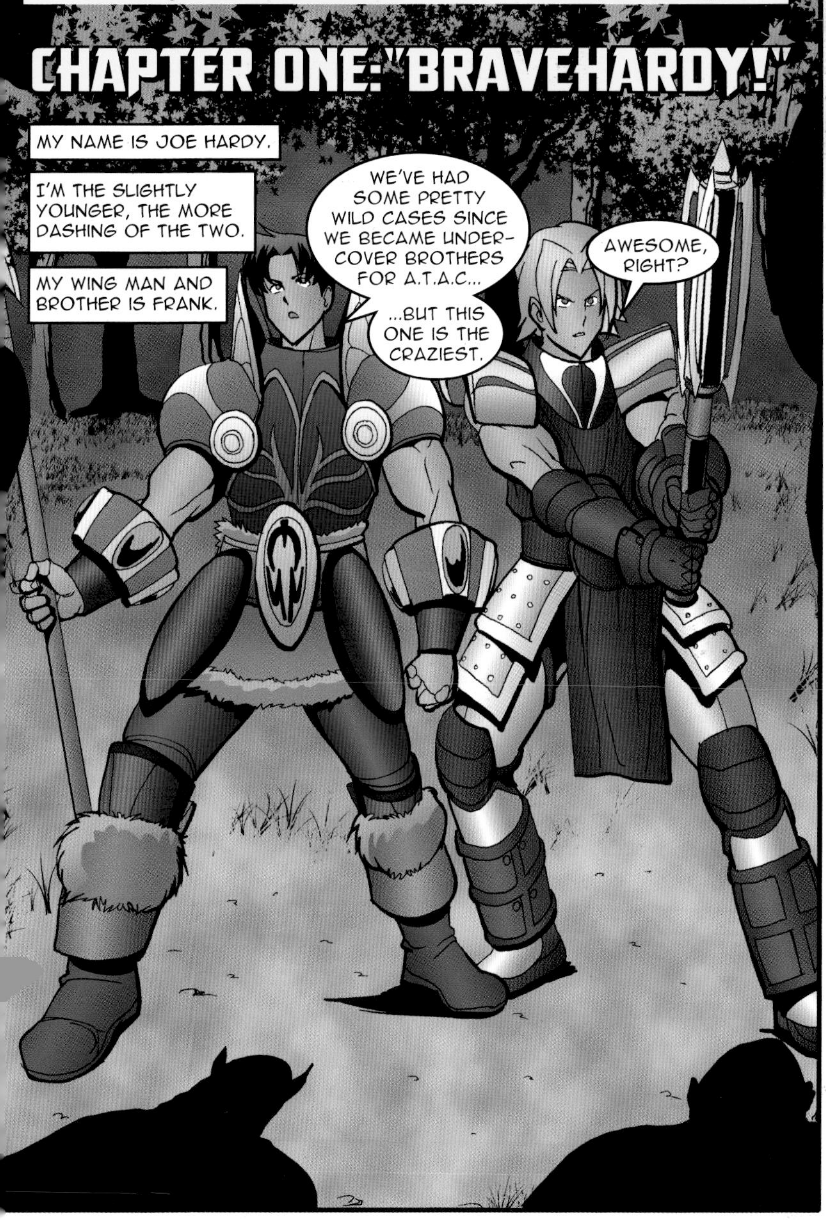
CHAPTER ONE: "BRAVEHARDY!"
MY NAME IS JOE HARDY.
I'M THE SLIGHTLY YOUNGER, THE MORE DASHING OF THE TWO.
MY WING MAN AND BROTHER IS FRANK.
WE'VE HAD SOME PRETTY WILD CASES SINCE WE BECAME UNDER-COVER BROTHERS FOR A.T.A.C...
...BUT THIS ONE IS THE CRAZIEST.
AWESOME, RIGHT?

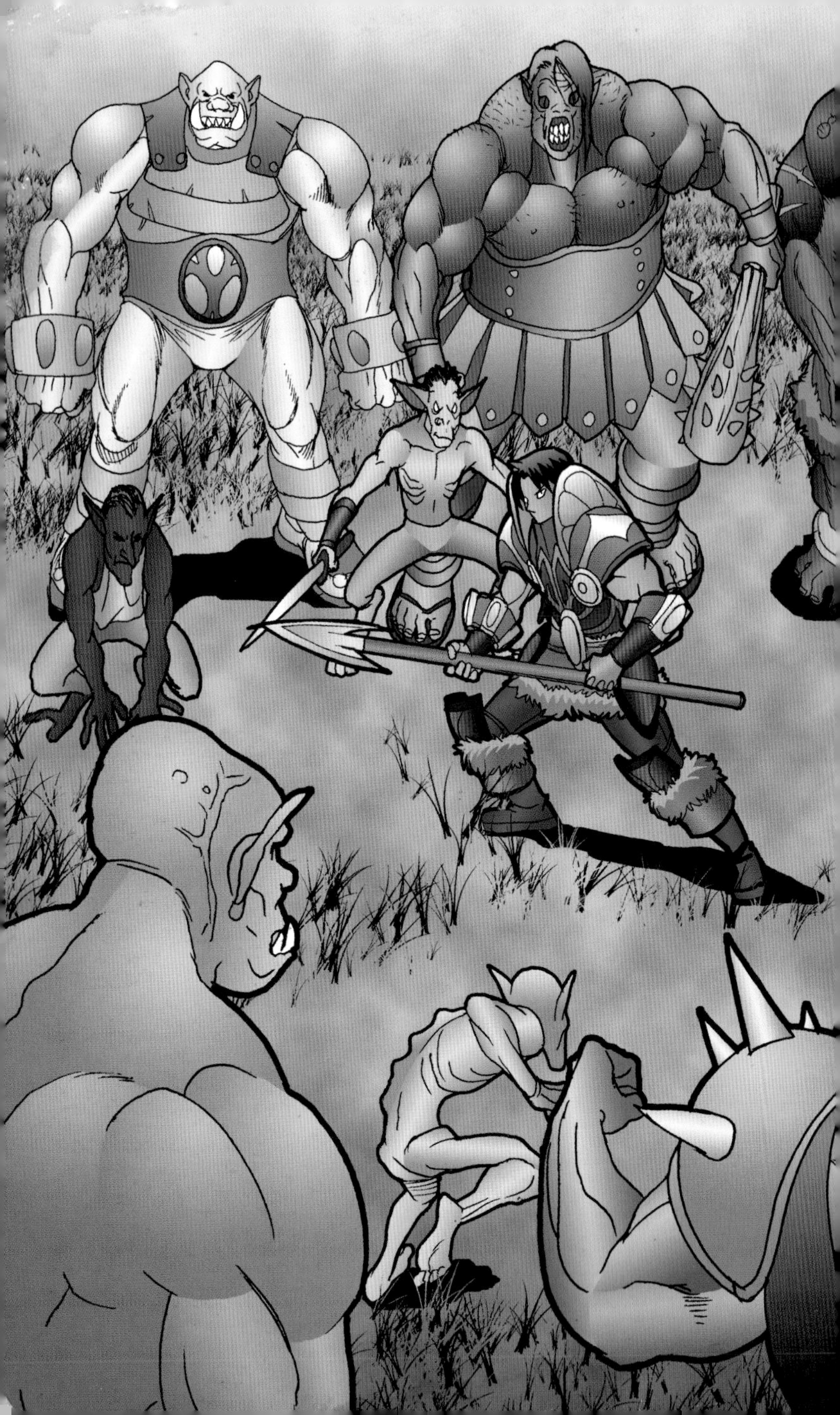

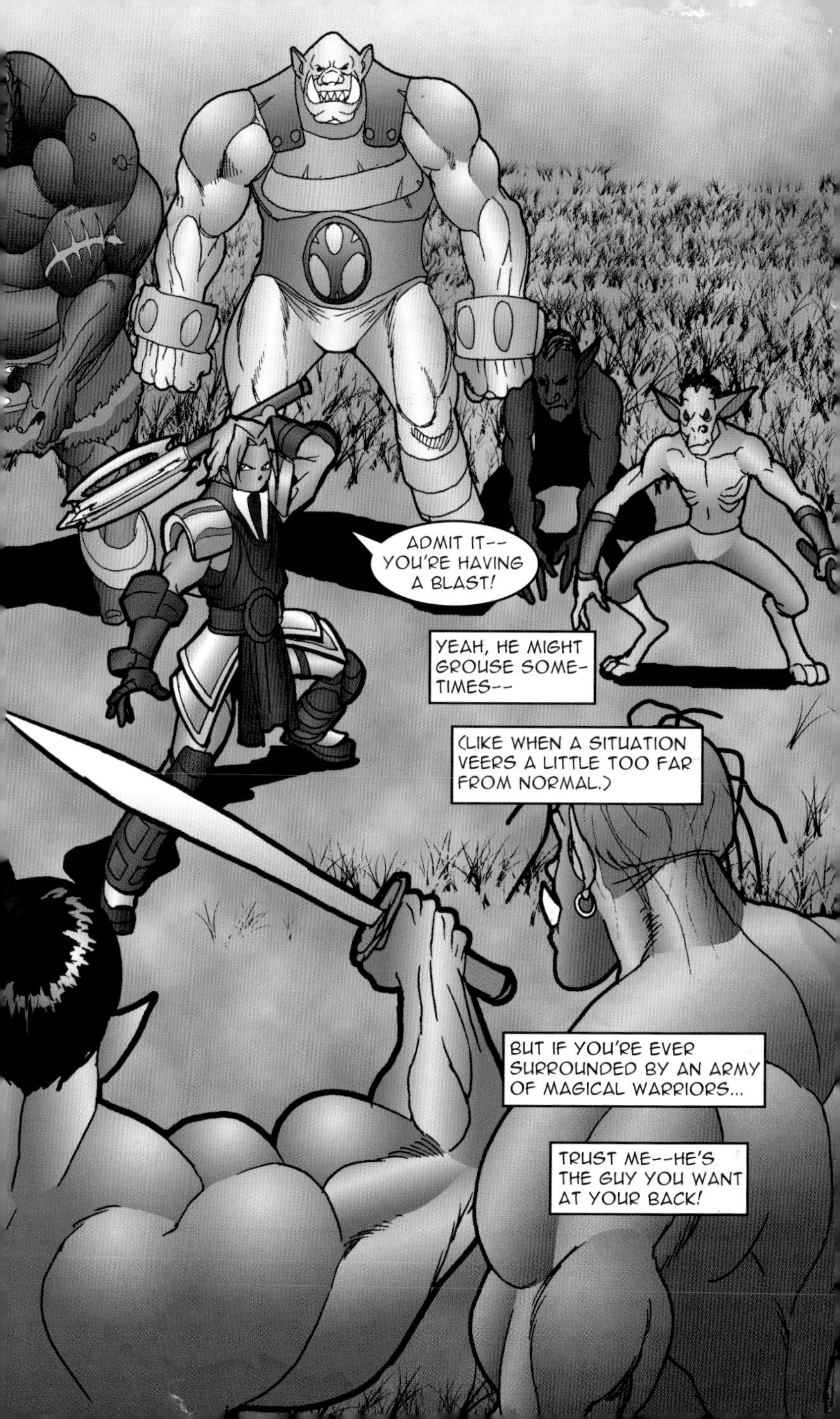
ADMIT IT--
YOU'RE HAVING
A BLAST!
YEAH, HE MIGHT
GROUSE SOME-
TIMES--
(LIKE WHEN A SITUATION
VEERS A LITTLE TOO FAR
FROM NORMAL.)
BUT IF YOU'RE EVER
SURROUNDED BY AN ARMY
OF MAGICAL WARRIORS...
TRUST ME--HE'S
THE GUY YOU WANT
AT YOUR BACK!

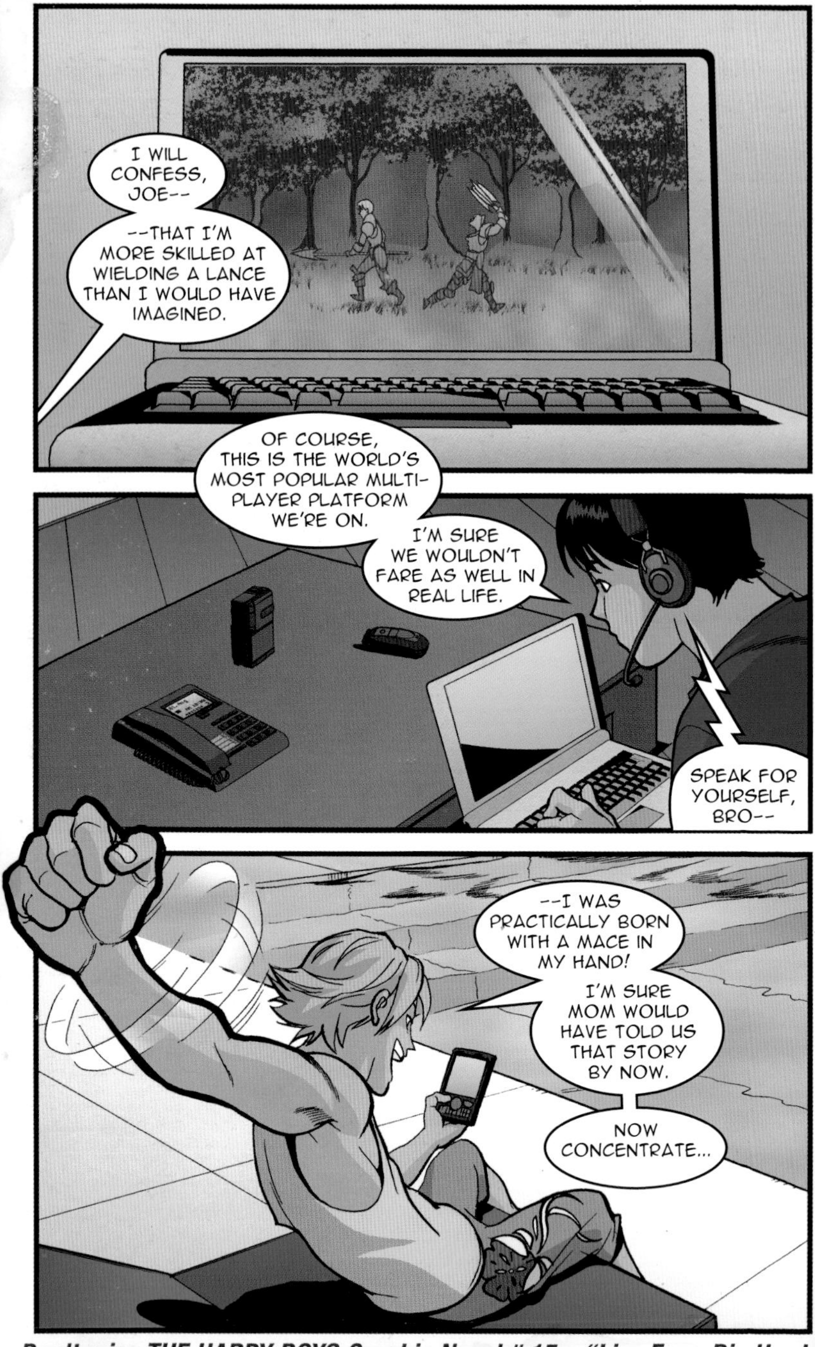
I WILL CONFESS, JOE--
--THAT I'M MORE SKILLED AT WIELDING A LANCE THAN I WOULD HAVE IMAGINED.
OF COURSE, THIS IS THE WORLD'S MOST POPULAR MULTI-PLAYER PLATFORM WE'RE ON.
I'M SURE WE WOULDN'T FARE AS WELL IN REAL LIFE.
SPEAK FOR YOURSELF, BRO--
--I WAS PRACTICALLY BORN WITH A MACE IN MY HAND!
I'M SURE MOM WOULD HAVE TOLD US THAT STORY BY NOW.
NOW CONCENTRATE...